The Incredible

of

Amanda

and

SKELLY

WOLFREN RIVERSTICK

First Edition

Copyright © Wolfren Riverstick 2007

Wolfren Riverstick has asserted the right under the Copyright, Designs and Patents Act, 1988, to be identified as the author of this work

British Library Cataloguing in Publication Data
A catalogue recording for this book is available from the British Library

ISBN 978-0-9554314-1-8

Cover illustration by Michelle Martin of Willowmoor Art Workshop, 76 Crackley Bank, Chesterton, Newcastle-under-Lyme

Book design by Antony Rowe Ltd

Typeset by Crazy Wolf Books, Worcestershire, England
Published by Crazy Wolf Books
www.crazywolfbooks.com

Printed and bound in England by Antony Rowe Ltd, Bumper's Farm, Chippenham, Wilts, SN14 6LH

For Robyn,

my favourite daughter,

with all of my love

CONTENTS

CHAPTER ONE

Moving House

"Here we are," announced Amanda's mum, rather triumphantly, as their car turned off the narrow country road into a driveway flanked on either side by stone pillars.

A pair of wrought-iron gates – in desperate need of a fresh lick of paint – hung precariously from the shabby, crumbling stonework of the pillars, which at one time would have been the entrance to a magnificent country house. However, Amanda thought that, judging by the current state of these structures, those grandiose days seemed to have faded into oblivion long ago. Her heart instantly sank as she studied the decaying pillars, wondering what kind of horror house they were going to be moving into which lay ahead of them at the far end of the driveway.

Once they were through the gates, Amanda's mother stopped the car and glanced back over her shoulder in the direction of the removal van that had been following her vehicle. Amanda also turned to face the same way and they both watched in silent anticipation, for several tense moments, while the pantechnicon struggled to squeeze between the pillars. After inching its way through, with nary a hair's breadth to spare, the large van eventually made it, and the small convoy set off again along the lengthy, winding driveway (more akin to a dirt track) that was full of potholes and fissures.

When they were halfway along the drive, Amanda happened to be looking out of the side window of the car when she thought she spotted a small figure dart between two trees, and then it was gone. She turned around to ask her mother whether she had seen it too, but Mum was looking in the rear-view mirror so Amanda did not bother to say anything. She thus put her supposed hallucination down to the fact that she was over-tired and imagining things. After puzzling about this for a few moments she pushed it to the back of her mind when the car finally drew to a halt in a circular, gravelled turning area outside the front entrance porch of the old mansion house.

"Isn't the house lovely, Amanda?" exclaimed her mother in an excited tone of voice. "I tried to describe to you how wonderful it was and it's exactly how I remember it to be. Well, you can decide for yourself... What do you think now that you can see it?"

"Huh! It's okay," Amanda sulked, seeming to be not in the least bit impressed, although she was secretly quite relieved because the house was in much better shape than the entrance pillars she had seen upon their initial arrival.

"Oh cheer up darling, you'll soon get to like it; I promise you will. It will be so much nicer living here than it was in that big city we left behind. What, with all those fumes from traffic and the pollution from chimneys.... and so many people too. Think how much healthier it will be for us here in the countryside."

"But what about all of my friends?" replied Amanda woefully, "I'll never see them again."

"You'll soon make new friends out here, and you will be starting your new school on Monday so in no time at all you'll have some new playmates," Mum replied.

The unhappy girl was not at all convinced and this showed in her facial expression. The scowl on Amanda's face failed to go unnoticed by her mother and she immediately tried to cheer up her daughter.

"Now that we've got a big garden with plenty of room how would you like it if Dad has a small stable block built, and then you could have that beloved horse or pony that you've always wanted?"

Suddenly Amanda appeared to be enthusiastic.

"A white horse?" she exclaimed.

Mum laughed.

"White, purple, pink, yellow – whatever colour you want!"

"Oh, thank you Mum," she said gleefully, and she threw her arms around her mother as she embraced her warmly.

"Well, at least that's cheered you up a bit," said Mum. "Let's go and take a look around now shall we?"

They got out of the car and began to walk towards the front door of the house but Mum was interrupted by the removal men, so she paused to give them instructions as to where she wanted them to put the household belongings. During the adults' conversation, Amanda soon became bored and she decided to wander off to explore the vast grounds of the house.

The garden was huge and mainly consisted of a lush emerald green lawn, in dire need of a good cut, which surrounded the whole house. It was full of plants and trees too, although they had become very overgrown because there had been nobody living at the property for a long time. At the rear of the house, the far end of the garden was enclosed by a high brick wall, in front of which there stood a small, tumbledown barn. Being of little interest to her, Amanda looked at the barn very briefly before turning to walk away but, at that precise moment, something caught her eye.

Swivelling swiftly around again, she glanced back at the old building but whatever she had spotted had already disappeared. Although Amanda was almost certain that she had seen it, she knew that it was also possible she may have only imagined seeing the small figure silhouetted in the doorway of the barn; however, this was the second time she had seen it in a short period of time and she thought it was too much to be a coincidence. Just then, whilst she pondered over this, a voice that came from directly behind her suddenly made Amanda jump out of her skin.

"Oh there you are darling. I wondered where you had got to."

Turning once more, Amanda quickly recovered from her scare when she realised it was only her mother.

"What's that old building Mum?" she asked, holding her hand over her chest to contain her racing heart.

"Well," answered Mum, pointing to the high brick wall, "in Victorian times that area would have been the kitchen garden, so I assume that the barn was a large potting shed where the gardeners used to store tools and seed.

"Many years ago a house of this size would have employed several gardeners who grew vegetables for the household all year round," she explained.

"I think that I saw something moving around over there," Amanda said excitedly.

"It was probably a stray cat or a rabbit, or maybe just your over-active imagination playing tricks on you," Mum said with a big grin on her face.

"No... It was bigger than a cat and a rabbit put together. Let's go and take a look."

As soon as she had finished saying this, Amanda eagerly set off across the lawn.

"Come back Amanda, there's nobody here except us and the removal men," Mum shouted after her. "There really is nothing to see. Besides, your father warned me to keep away from the barn because it is not very safe…so come back here this minute!"

Amanda stopped running and shrugged her shoulders in frustration.

"Please let me take a look," she pleaded.

"No!"

"Oh Mum," groaned Amanda, at the same time stamping her feet in temper.

"Stop being such a spoilt baby just because you can't get your own way. Now come along, I want to show you around the house."

Mum began to walk towards the house and – pulling a face like a constipated hippopotamus might do – Amanda reluctantly headed back across the lawn, casting occasional glances over her shoulder towards the barn. All of a sudden, the ramshackle outbuilding really did seem more interesting than the boring old house because she was intrigued by the thought of something lurking within. Nevertheless, Amanda followed her mother into the house.

Their new home was much larger than the one they had left behind in the city – in fact, the ground floor alone was bigger than both levels of their previous house put together. To begin with, a heavy solid oak front door opened into an immense hallway that contained a beautiful tiled floor – finished in crimson, black and white. Leading off the hallway were two living rooms with gaping fireplaces which, Amanda discovered, were big enough for her to stand upright in. And then there was a kitchen, the likes of which Amanda had never seen before, except in glossy magazine pictures of stately homes. The inside of the property had only just been renovated by a local construction firm and the smell of fresh paint still lingered in the air, so Amanda's mum opened all of the big sash windows in every room as they passed through the ground floor in order to let the odour of paint fumes escape.

A broad, winding staircase led from the hallway to an enormous galleried landing with access to seven bedrooms and the most luxurious bathroom Amanda had ever set eyes upon. Here, a king-size bath with clumsy-looking cast-iron feet stood alone in the centre of the room, its gold-plated taps casting a lustrous reflection upon the newly-enamelled bath surface.

"The four bedrooms at the end of the landing will be guest rooms for whenever we have any visitors staying over," explained Mum, "and they all have en-suite bathrooms too."

"This will be your playroom," Mum continued as she opened the door next to the bathroom. "Here you can play away to your heart's content with your numerous toys and games and I won't have to worry about picking them up after you."

Amanda's mouth hung open in awe, but before she had time to say a word she was quickly whisked away to the adjoining room.

"And this is your bedroom," Mum proudly announced.

"It's huge!" squealed Amanda in delight.

Without saying anything further, she quickly ran across the floor to peer out of the window which overlooked the rear garden with its high brick wall that separated it from the fields beyond. There was a perfect view of the tumbledown barn from Amanda's bedroom window and, as she stared at the building, she felt there was definitely something odd about it. Determined to find out, she was sure that she would get to the bottom of whatever it was eventually.

"There's a small vanity bathroom en-suite as well, just in case you get caught short in the middle of the night," Mum said with a grin.

"Wow! This house is just like a fairytale palace," Amanda exclaimed.

"There you are, you see; I knew you would like it once you had seen the inside... I am pleased."

Then, a man's voice – that came from somewhere on the galleried landing – suddenly brought their conversation to an abrupt halt.

"Excuse me for interrupting," said the removal man, "but would you mind if we started to bring your furniture upstairs now? We've finished unloading on the ground floor and it won't take long to cart the rest of your kit up here."

"Of course you can," replied Mum. "In the meantime, I'll try to find the kettle and make you all a cup of tea."

"That's a great idea missus. I'm pretty sure the lads are all gagging for a cuppa... I know that I am."

"Please bring the boxes marked 'TOYS' up to the playroom first – Amanda will show you which room that is."

"Will do," replied the removal man, and then he redirected his conversation towards Amanda. "Lead the way then lassie and we'll get on the case right away."

"As soon as the men bring your stuff up you can begin to unpack straight away, Amanda," said Mum, as she set off down the stairs in her quest to locate the kettle.

"That should keep you occupied and out of harm's way until your father gets home," she added as an afterthought.

Amanda's father was called Bill, and he worked in the city of London. She really had no idea exactly what he did there but she believed that he had offices and lots of people worked for him. He would probably be late home from work now that they would be living in the countryside because he had much further to travel than he used to have to their previous home in the city.

Sure enough, it was six-thirty that evening when her dad arrived home from work and, as soon as Amanda heard the sound of his car engine, she ran outside to greet him; she was always pleased to see him. As usual, he hoisted her off the ground until she was looking directly into his eyes.

"How's my favourite daughter?" asked Dad.

Then he gave her a big kiss on the cheek and placed her back down on the ground. Amanda put her hands on her hips and emitted a long-suffering sigh.

"Dad… I'm your only daughter!" she informed him.

Her father placed his right hand over his right eye and looked around him.

"Oh yes, so you are," he agreed, and they both laughed.

This was a routine they often went through together and it had become an expected tradition.

"Where's Tabs?" asked Amanda, a worried frown suddenly appearing on her face.

'Tabs' was the name of Amanda's two-year-old cat – a British silver tabby – who had spent the previous night and all of that day in a cattery whilst they moved into the new house.

Dad tapped the side of his head with his index finger after she had put this question to him.

"Oh no! I knew there was something I had forgotten," he said, but when he realised that Amanda was about to burst into tears he added more to his comment. "I'm just kidding. She's in the car really. Come along, let's go and fetch her out and introduce her to her new surroundings."

Tabs hated travelling in cars and she seemed extremely happy just to get out of the vehicle. The cat made a huge fuss of Amanda, as if she had not seen her owner for more than a month, purring excitedly and nestling comfortably into her arms. Amanda beamed at her father.

"Look, she's pleased to see me," she said.

"Wouldn't you be if you had been locked in a cage all day long?" said Dad. "Let's take her into the house now and give her a bone!"

"She's a cat, not a dog, silly," Amanda said scornfully, but she laughed all the same because she realised that he was joking around. He always said stupid things to her and she liked that because he often made her chuckle.

Amanda told her father how much she liked the new house but the only bad point was that she would miss her friends. In answer to that, Dad gave her a big hug, assuring her that she would soon make new friends, and then he accompanied her into the living room.

"Hello Janet," he said. "The traffic was terrible travelling out of the city, but I suppose I'll have to get used to it."

"You'll definitely have to get used to it," his wife replied. "I'm not moving home again in a hurry. What an exhausting day!"

"You seem to have got everything pretty much in order though," he said, looking all around. "It looks great."

"Well, the removal men did the donkey work – they certainly earn their money. In fact, they only left here a short while ago."

"I know. I had to pull onto the grass verge to let their van pass by along the lane."

"I've only had enough time to sort out the bare necessities so far," Mum continued, "but there's still an awful lot to do and it will be days before we're back to some sort of normality."

"These things take time… Rome wasn't built in a day, as they say."

"Dad, when can I have a horse?" Amanda interrupted. "Mum says that we have enough space here to have one now."

"As soon as the stable is built you can have a horse," Dad replied.

"When will that be?"

"Oh, in about three years' time I expect."

Amanda looked disappointed.

"I'm only joking," Dad said with a grin on his face. "Give me a chance to settle in, for goodness sake! We've only moved in today so I haven't had much time to think about it yet. Hopefully, in just a few weeks, we'll have your precious stable built for you… At this particular moment though, it's time for you to get ready for bed young lady. It's been a long day and we're all tired. I'll come upstairs to tuck you in when you're ready."

"But it's only seven o'clock and we haven't eaten dinner yet!" Amanda complained.

"Dinner's on its way," shouted Mum, who was heading in the direction of the kitchen at that very moment.

"I'm sorry Amanda," Dad apologised. "It has been a long day and I seem to have lost all track of time; thank goodness it's the weekend now. Okay, I stand corrected… after you have eaten you are allowed one hour to let your meal digest and then you can get ready for bed. Does that sound like a better deal?"

"That's much more like it," Amanda agreed.

"*Come and get it!*" Mum's voice wafted in from the kitchen.

"Let's go and wash our hands before we eat," said Dad. "Race you to the sink….where is the sink by the way?"

Amanda had already taken off before he had even finished his sentence and, of course, she beat him to the kitchen sink because she was already getting used to their new house and knew exactly where to locate it.

When dinner was over Amanda went up to her bedroom to finish arranging her cuddly toys. Then she had a bath, combed her hair, brushed her teeth and was in bed by eight-thirty sharp, without messing around like she normally did.

"What's this, a new world record?" said her father when he poked his head around Amanda's bedroom door. "It usually takes up to an hour for you to get into bed after you've been sent there… I can't believe that moving house is what it takes to make you turn over a new leaf."

"I'm in bed early because I'm tired," said Amanda, blinking her eyes drowsily. "I think I shall dream about white horses all night long," she managed to say between yawns as her father tucked in the bedclothes. "Goodnight."

Dad then bent forward in order to give his daughter a kiss whilst, at the same time, she raised her head to meet him halfway. After that, she yawned once more and then Amanda was asleep before her head had even fallen back onto the pillow.

CHAPTER TWO

The Mystery within the Old Barn

Amanda's first weekend in her new house flew swiftly by, with most of her time being taken up in assisting her mother to unpack their worldly goods and with sorting out her own belongings. Then, on the following Monday, Amanda started her new school. Sherbourne Hills Refectory School was a quaint, old-fashioned building – more like a Victorian country manor than a school – and much smaller than her old one in the city, with not so many pupils either. Everyone seemed very friendly there and it did not take her at all long to get acquainted and make new friends. However, the school was in the village of Darwood, about three miles from Amanda's home, and, because most of the pupils lived in the village, it was difficult for Amanda to bring friends home to keep her company. Therefore, she spent most of her evenings alone in her playroom during that first week, which made her feel quite lonely at times.

One particularly stuffy night Amanda found that she could not get off to sleep because it was too warm in her bedroom, so she got out of bed to open her window. It was a bright, moonlit night and, as she reached for the window latch, she spotted a small figure flit across the garden before disappearing beneath the dark shadows cast by the trees. Believing that she was seeing things, Amanda waited patiently, watching to see if the mysterious figure reappeared. Sure enough, after a few seconds, there it was again and then it vanished once more, darting to and fro in a zigzag pattern across the lawn. In the pale blue moonlight, Amanda noticed that the figure appeared to shimmer – like sunlight dancing on water – but when it was in the shadows it vanished altogether, and she was bewitched by this.

For a short while she remained frozen to the spot, totally mesmerised by this spectacle, as she wondered what could possibly make the unknown figure glisten in the moonlight. All she knew was that whoever – or whatever – the figure was, it appeared to be heading towards the back door of the house. It occurred to her that this thing might be dangerous but, although she felt a little frightened, Amanda thought that she would investigate all the same. So, she crept very quietly down the stairs on tiptoes for she was afraid that she might disturb the intruder before she had a chance to take a good look at it. Amanda was full of curiosity and did not know what she would do if she came face-to-face with the mystery figure, but if she was attacked then she would scream the house down in order to wake up her parents.

The house was in darkness; however, as she entered the hallway, Amanda could see a thin beam of light coming from the kitchen because the door was slightly ajar. She approached cautiously, one of her trembling hands grasping a torch that she had not switched on as yet whilst, in her other hand, she clutched her favourite teddy bear close to her chest which gave her a sense of security. When she reached the kitchen, she peered warily through the gap in the doorway and then realised that someone had left the refrigerator door open and that was where the light was coming from. Thankfully, there was no sign of any intruder in the kitchen and she breathed a grateful sigh of relief.

Having relaxed at this point, Amanda walked across the kitchen floor and closed the refrigerator door, but then it was quite dark. She immediately switched on her torch and shone it around the room, searching for the light switch. At that precise moment, something brushed past her at lightning speed, which caused the surprised girl to drop both the torch and her teddy bear at the same instance. Amanda's initial surprise turned to panic as soon as this had happened and she began to scream at the top of her voice, while whatever had touched her rapidly shot through the cat flap and out into the garden. Her high-pitched screams had the desired effect and, once the alarm was raised, Amanda's parents were at her side in a trice.

"Whatever is the matter with you Amanda? Have you been sleepwalking?" asked Mum in a rather concerned voice.

"No, I haven't been sleepwalking. There was something in here and I came to have a look," Amanda sobbed.

Her parents glanced worriedly around the kitchen.

"There is nobody here except for us," Mum reassured her in a positive tone of voice. "The back door is still locked – I've tried the handle – so it is impossible for someone else to be in our house."

"It wasn't s-someone, it was s-something!" stammered Amanda. "And it was definitely here, I saw it with my own two eyes. It touched me too and then flew out of the cat flap before I could get a good look at it."

"I'll go and take a look around, just to be on the safe side," said Dad. With that, he hurriedly set off to search around the house.

In no time at all though, he returned empty-handed.

"There is definitely nobody else here," he confirmed, raising his arms in despair. "Look, the back door is securely locked and I have the key in my hand, therefore no-one can get in or out."

Dad pulled and tugged at the door handle to prove his point to Amanda.

"You've just had a bad dream love. Come along now, back to bed," said Mum, and then she led Amanda towards her bedroom.

"I'll leave the landing light on for you just for tonight to make you feel safer," she said. "Sweet dreams."

Mum pulled the covers over her daughter, kissed her on the cheek and then returned to her own bedroom. Moments later, Tabs leapt onto Amanda's bed and began kneading her pillow, at the same time purring noisily away into Amanda's left ear. The tired young girl sluggishly raised one of her arms and reached out to stroke the cat.

"There was definitely something in the kitchen Tabs," she whispered. "I know there was. I don't know how yet, but one way or another I'll find out exactly what it was."

Tabs simply blinked idly at Amanda through half-open eyelids before curling up beside her and very soon they had both drifted off into the land of Nod.

The next day was Saturday and Amanda appeared to be none the worse for her previous night's experience when she came downstairs at breakfast time. In actual fact, she had more or less forgotten all about it.

"Would you like cereal for breakfast Amanda?" asked Mum.

In answer to this, Amanda nodded her head as she sat down at the table, so her mother then went over to the refrigerator to fetch a bottle of milk; but when she returned there was a concerned frown upon her face.

"You're drinking an awful lot of milk lately," she said to Amanda. "It's not good for you in such a great quantity you know."

"I haven't had a glass of milk for ages," remarked Amanda in complete astonishment.

"Well, there were two pints in the fridge last night but, all of a sudden, it has gone... Go and see if the milkman has been yet, otherwise you will have to go without breakfast."

Amanda looked hurt.

"It wasn't me – I didn't drink all of the milk," she said scornfully.

"So, it was that mysterious Mr Nobody again I suppose," Mum retorted. "Now, stop arguing and do as you're told... go and see if the milkman has been."

Amanda dutifully arose from the table, for she was not in the right mood for an argument. Meanwhile, while this conversation was taking place, her father had been filling in the crossword of a daily newspaper, just like he did every morning. He looked up from his task and watched Amanda leave the room before speaking.

"If Amanda didn't drink the milk, then who did?" he uttered.

"I've no idea," said his wife. "Perhaps Amanda drank the milk in her sleepwalking state last night, although it's hard to believe that would have been possible because there were no empty bottles or glasses left lying about."

"Hmm," grunted Dad with a puzzled expression on his face. "I think I will fit some new security bolts to the back door today Janet... just for peace of mind."

"That's probably a good idea anyway," she agreed. Then there was a brief silence before she changed the subject. "I'm going into town later today to do some shopping, are you coming with me?"

"I don't think so. I've got too much to do here and if I don't make a start the jobs will never get done," replied her husband.

At that moment, Amanda returned with two bottles of milk. She handed them to her mother and pulled up a chair at the table.

"Is that all there is?" asked Mum in genuine surprise. "That's odd. I actually ordered three pints because it's the weekend and there is no delivery on Sunday. I can only assume that the milkman must have forgotten to leave an extra pint. Oh, well… When you've finished breakfast get ready to come into town with me".

Amanda looked disappointed and began to protest.

"Oh Mum, can't I stay here and play? You know I hate shopping – it's so boring!"

"No, your father is busy; you'll have to come with me."

"She can stay here with me if that's what she wants," said Dad, "so long as she doesn't wander off. Besides, I shan't be far away."

"Thanks Dad, I promise I'll be good," said a jubilant Amanda as she jumped up from her chair and rushed around the table to give her father a loving hug.

Mum left the house at noon and, after Amanda had watched the car disappear down the long driveway, she approached her father.

"Please can I go outside to play now, Dad?"

"You most certainly may, the fresh air will be good for you. I'll be out to do some jobs in a short while, when I've finished my office work."

"Thanks Dad."

"Don't go out of the garden though," yelled her father as Amanda hurriedly bolted through the front door.

"Don't worry, I won't," came her reply, which was virtually drowned out by a loud bang as the heavy oak door slammed shut.

As it turned out, Amanda had no intention of leaving the garden anyway because she had more important things on her mind. She had been yearning to explore the interior of the old barn since moving in and, with her mum now safely out of the way and Dad busy with his office work, this was a golden opportunity not to be missed.

When she first went outside she played with her skipping rope – an extremely rare occurrence now that she was getting older – gradually working her way across the garden towards the barn. Every once in a while Amanda's father would peep through the living room window to make sure that she was safe and, every time he looked in her direction, Amanda waved to him to let him know that she was doing fine. After a short time though, he stopped checking up on her, and this was just what she had been waiting for because, when she knew that she was no longer under the watchful gaze of her father, Amanda darted into the barn.

Once inside, she found that the upper floor and ceiling had fallen in long ago, which allowed narrow slivers of daylight to filter through the broken roof tiles to the ground below. However, coming directly from the bright sunlight into the dark interior of the barn meant that Amanda had to wait for her eyes to become accustomed to the darkness because it would never do to fall over an obstacle and injure herself. Only when she could begin to make out the outline of certain objects around her did she begin to examine the room, whereupon she noticed that the floor was littered with a variety of items, all covered in dust and grime that had built-up over the years. There was an ancient-looking tea chest for a start, a tatty old suitcase, several crates and boxes, a broken-down table, chairs with legs missing, and piles of newspapers and magazines were strewn all over the place. In fact, all manner of junk filled the room.

Trembling at the thought of what she might find, Amanda began to search through the piles of junk, disturbing clouds of dust particles that tickled her nostrils and made her feel like sneezing. She gingerly tipped over the lid of the ancient tea chest, to discover that it was full of empty milk bottles which had been covered with a handful of dirty old rags. Then she looked inside the numerous boxes and crates and found that these were crammed full of used milk bottles too.

After that, the only place remaining which needed to be investigated was the inside of the suitcase, whose lid was closed but its catches were unclasped. Amanda slowly raised the lid and, at the very moment that she did so, it suddenly flew out of her hands as something scrambled out of the case. Her first opinion was that the 'something' appeared to be a kind of creature, for it was certainly not an animal and therefore this was the only word she could think of to describe it.

Amanda stepped backwards in fright, tumbling over the objects that were scattered all around her and falling flat on her back. In the meantime, the creature was bouncing off the walls of the barn as it raced around the place looking for somewhere to hide. Eventually, it came to rest in a dark corner where it thought that it could no longer be seen.

"W-w-who are you?" stammered Amanda, when she had finally managed to find her voice, but there was no reply.

"W-w-what are you?" she asked, edging her way towards the open doorway and tripping over yet another obstacle.

The creature simply cowered in the corner, quiet and still. This eerie silence was all too much for Amanda to bear and, springing to her feet, she rushed out of the door and into the garden as quickly as her legs would take her – and not until she was halfway across the garden lawn and as far away from the barn as possible did she stop running. It was only at this point that she cast a backwards glance toward the barn and realised she was perfectly safe, so she paused to regain her breath whilst taking a few moments to think about what had just taken place.

"Well, it didn't attack me, and neither did it follow me, so I assume that it must be harmless," she muttered out loud. "In fact, now that I think about it, the creature seemed to be more frightened of me than I was of it! In that case, I'll go and get a torch so that I can have a good look at it."

Rather foolishly, Amanda had not even thought about taking a torch with her on that first visit to the barn; but she was intending to be fully equipped on her next visit, so she rushed into the house to collect a powerful flashlight that her father kept in a bathroom cabinet. Then, upon returning to the front door, she almost collided with her father who had left his office and stepped into the hallway to see why Amanda was making such a racket.

"Hey, steady on young lady! What's all the commotion about?" he asked.

Amanda hid the flashlight behind her back.

"Oh, it's nothing to worry about, Dad," she guiltily replied. "I was just getting something else to play with."

"Hmmm," Dad grunted disbelievingly. "Just calm down a little – You're behaving like a bull in a china shop."

Having said all that he wanted to say, Dad turned around and went back to his office. Then, remembering to shut the door quietly behind her, Amanda sped across the lawn and slipped back into the barn unnoticed by her father. Shaking like a leaf, she shone the flashlight into the corner of the room and found that the strange creature was still there, in exactly the same spot as where she had last seen it. In an attempt to shield its eyes from the bright beam of light, the creature instinctively raised its arms in the air and covered its face with its hands.

After drenching the creature with light, an awestruck Amanda could now establish exactly what she was confronted with. At first glance, the creature's body resembled that of a skeleton because its bones were clearly visible, but after a closer inspection it was plain to see that its skeletal frame was in fact covered with a transparent, jelly-like flesh. Its skin glistened in the torchlight and, from this, Amanda deduced that here was the very thing she had seen flit across the moonlit garden on the previous night and enter the house. It greatly satisfied her to know that she had not dreamt the whole episode as her mother had suggested.

The girl had already estimated the creature's height to be approximately two feet and it was not until she diverted the beam of light away from the creature's face that it lowered its arms to reveal its facial features. She then found herself staring into the most enormous saucer-shaped eyes you could ever imagine, cobalt blue in colour, which blinked lazily as if they were operating in slow motion. It had the tiniest button nose you ever did see and a wide mouth that curled upwards at each end to give the appearance of a constant smile, whilst there were elfin-like, pointed ears on either side of its perfectly round head. Finally, perched on top of the creature's head was a tuft of fur that appeared to be as fine as silk as well as being transparent, just like the strands of a fibre-optic lamp. The creature's overall appearance was most unusual to say the least but Amanda thought it seemed quite cute, regardless of how it looked. So, feeling certain that this little fellow was harmless, Amanda began to move cautiously towards it.

"Don't be afraid," she said in a gentle whisper. "I won't harm you as long as you don't harm me."

After saying this, she slowly reached out her hand to touch the creature's strange-looking flesh, and it came as no real surprise for Amanda to learn that it really did feel like jelly, although the fact that it felt warm was the odd part.

"What are you, and how did you get to be living here in this old building?" she asked.

The creature still made no attempt to answer, nor did it try to move away from her.

"Well, you obviously don't speak, so how are we going to communicate?"

Amanda felt frustrated but she managed to smile all the same. Then, to her amazement, the creature unexpectedly returned a welcoming grin of its own.

"Are you hungry or thirsty?" Amanda said excitedly, pleased that she had made a small breakthrough at last, and she pointed towards her mouth using hand signals to indicate that she was eating food.

The creature wore a puzzled expression at first, but then a smile broke out on its face again, followed by a repeated nodding of its head. But, before she could advance any further with her one-sided conversation, Amanda suddenly heard the distant sound of her father's voice as he called out her name.

"Oh dear," she told the creature, "I will be in big trouble if my dad finds me in here. I shall have to go now but I promise to come back later with some food and drink, so don't go away."

With the sound of her father's voice growing ever nearer, Amanda stood up to leave. When she got to the doorway of the barn she turned around and shone the flashlight at the creature, just to take one more look.

"Goodbye," she whispered, and the creature smiled at her once more.

At that point, Amanda made a hurried departure.

CHAPTER THREE

Amanda Discovers a Whole New World

When Amanda left the barn she saw her father pacing up and down the lawn and heard him shouting her name at the top of his voice. Then, as soon as he caught sight of his daughter, he stormed towards her with his face as black as a thunder cloud. Having witnessed this dark scowl on more than one occasion in the past, Amanda knew that she was in deep trouble so she braced herself ready for a verbal onslaught.

"Where have you been?" Dad ranted. "I've been looking everywhere for you. I'm extremely busy and I've got better things to do than chase all over the countryside looking for you. Your mother has returned home from her shopping trip and she's getting tea ready, so you had better come in now... Look at the state of you – you're filthy! Go and wash your hands immediately."

"Yes Dad," said Amanda, rather sheepishly, and she dodged past her father to disappear into the house, counting her blessings that she had got off so lightly.

Later on, when Amanda had finished her evening meal, she offered to help out with the kitchen chores of her own free will. Part of her daily routine was to load the dishwasher, a task that only took a few minutes and one that she loathed doing, which she was forever trying to find a way out of, but on this particular night she was trying to get back into her parents' good books and earn some much-needed Brownie points. The reason for this was because she was desperate to return to the barn and see the strange creature again. Time seemed to drag by very slowly but eventually the chores were done and Amanda's mother gave her permission to go outside for no more than an hour.

As quick as a lightning flash, Amanda was out of the door and halfway across the garden when she remembered that she had earlier promised the creature something to eat and drink. Muttering and cursing under her breath she turned around and raced back into the house, almost colliding with her father in her haste yet again.

"Hey! Hey! Slow down young lady," he shouted. "That's the second time today that you've nearly knocked me flying. What on Earth has got into you lately?"

"Sorry Dad," said Amanda, but she did not stop to explain what she was up to, of course.

When Amanda reached the kitchen her mum was still in there so it was going to be impossible to sneak refreshments out of the house unnoticed.

"Can I have a can of pop and some chocolate biscuits please Mum?" Amanda asked, with the sweetest of smiles on her face.

"Surely you can't still be hungry after that great big meal you ate tonight!"

"It's not for me, it's for my fluffy toys – we're having a party," said Amanda, hating to have to tell a lie.

Mum laughed.

"Yes I'm sure it is," she said disbelievingly. "Go on then, but not

31

too many biscuits mind – you will be going to bed shortly and it's not good for you to sleep on a full stomach."

"Thanks," said Amanda, grabbing a plateful of biscuits and a can of pop before her mother had even finished saying her sentence.

Then she dashed out of the house again and ran across the lawn, but she failed to see Tabs curled up fast asleep in the long grass and she tripped over the poor cat, which sent the chocolate biscuits flying in all directions. Following this rude awakening, Tabs leapt into the air, hissing and spitting at Amanda in temper.

"Sorry Tabs, but you really should look where you are going," Amanda scalded whilst gathering up the spilled biscuits.

Tabs looked at Amanda through squinted eyes as if she understood what had been said to her but could not believe that she was taking the blame for her owner's mistake. And then, after blinking warily at the girl, she stole away in a huff to let Amanda continued on her way unhindered.

When she reached the barn, Amanda had to fumble around inside the doorway for a brief while as she searched for her flashlight, until eventually locating it on the ground just inside the doorway. Still fumbling, she then flicked the switch that brought it to life and entered the barn to find the strange-looking creature in exactly the same place as where she had last seen it during her previous visit.

"It's only me," she whispered softly. "I'm back. Look, I've brought you some fizzy pop and a plateful of biscuits."

The creature surveyed the offering but it did not seem at all interested in partaking.

"What's the matter? Don't you want it?"

The creature shook its head.

"Milk…" it said.

"*SO, YOU DO SPEAK!*" said the flabbergasted girl.

"Milk…" repeated the creature.

"But I only have pop – It's just as good," Amanda insisted.

The creature shook its head again.

"Oh, very well then, I'll go and fetch some milk instead," she surrendered.

Once again she ran back to the house, on this occasion to swap the can of pop for a glass of milk. Fortunately for her, Amanda's mother had vacated the kitchen so she helped herself to a glass of milk without having to give an explanation for this. With this task accomplished, she hurriedly returned to the barn and handed the glass to the creature, who demolished the white liquid in an instant.

"Ah, that's just what I needed," gasped the creature, and then it belched repeatedly.

"*I beg your pardon!*"

"Pardon me," came the polite apology.

"I should think so too! My goodness, you must have been thirsty," she exclaimed, and then she watched in amazement as the creature's jelly-like flesh suddenly turned white and its bones were no longer visible.

"Wh… What's happening to you?" asked Amanda in a frightened voice.

"Don't be scared, for there really is nothing to be afraid of," the creature told her. "The milk is merely restoring my body to its natural colour."

Amanda breathed a sigh of relief and began to talk nineteen to the dozen.

"Who are you?" she gabbled. "What kind of creature are you? Are you a boy or a girl?"

"I'm a boy," he replied, "and I'm not a creature, I'm a being."

"Do you have a name?" was her next question.

"My name is Star-Kid-Explorer-Lost-Lotsa-Years..."

Amanda's mouth dropped open in astonishment.

"...but everyone knows me as Skelly," he said with a grin.

"Thank goodness for that! What an awfully long name, I would never be able to say the first one that you said."

"My name is really an acronym – formed from the capital letters of each word in my name – that reads as SKELLY... See?"

"Yes, I understand," said Amanda.

"Actually, I made the acronym bit up; I've had a lot of time to do stuff like that you see. The truth is, where I come from everyone is called SKELLY."

"Gosh! Doesn't that get confusing?"

"No, not at all. It seems to work out alright but don't ask me how. Anyway, I've told you my name but you haven't told me yours yet."

"I'm called Amanda – no fancy acra... acri... acru... whatever it's called – just plain old Amanda."

"Pleased to meet you Amanda," said Skelly, holding out one of his hands. Amanda grabbed it and gave a firm handshake.

"Me too... I think," she faltered. Understandably, she was still a little unsure at this point.

"So, if you are a being – and you're obviously not a human being – where do you come from?"

Skelly pointed towards the Heavens.

"I come from the skies," he proudly announced.

Raising her head upwards, Amanda stared at the patches of evening sky that could be seen through the numerous holes in the roof. After a few moments she lowered her head and opened her mouth to speak again but nothing came out and she simply stared at Skelly in disbelief.

"I know that seems hard to believe but it's absolutely true," Skelly assured her. "In actual fact, I come from a sweet little planet known as Laktose, which is located many miles away from here in a place known as the Milky Way. So that makes me an alien being in effect."

It took a while but Amanda eventually found her voice again.

"If that's the case, then how did you get here?" she enquired.

"I fell to Earth in a space-egg."

"*A space-egg!* What the heck is a space-egg?" Amanda queried.

"It's a travelling capsule, not much larger than that thing over there," replied Skelly, pointing to the battered old suitcase that he liked to sleep in.

"Have you been here – on Earth I mean – for very long?"

"Yes, about fifty or sixty years at a guess."

"*Fifty or sixty years!* That's an extremely long time. You don't look that old."

"Time means nothing to me because we never grow old on the planet Laktose."

"Why didn't you return to your own planet?"

Skelly suddenly appeared to be quite downcast.

"Unfortunately, my space-egg was damaged when it crash-landed here and I couldn't repair it because technology didn't exist here on your planet in those bygone days. I don't even know whether the correct technology to enable my return exists even now – I reckon that it might do though, judging by the modern gadgets that I have seen in some houses. All the same, I have never asked anyone about this subject because it is not safe to talk to people."

"Why ever not?" Amanda interrupted.

"Because I will be taken away by men in white coats who will carry out all sorts of strange, nasty experiments on me once they know that I am an alien being."

"Then why are you talking to me?" she enquired.

"Because I sense that you are a safe person to talk to. You are a lonely child just like me... I have not spoken to anyone for many years."

"You poor thing," Amanda said sympathetically. "Don't you have any friends?"

"The last friend that I had was a boy named Ted. He used to live in this house when I first ended up here."

"That was years ago," Amanda began, "and that would make him an old man now."

"Yes, you're right; Ted would indeed be an old man now. He grew up in the house that you now live in but I didn't see much of him as he became older, and then he moved away for good. There have been other occupants since, but the house has been empty for at least the last twenty-five years."

"And you've been here all alone for twenty-five years with nobody to talk to? That's so sad... and you must miss your family terribly."

"Yes," said Skelly, wiping a tear from his eye. "But, perhaps, one day soon I will be able to go home."

"Let's hope so... I know, maybe we can fix your space-egg," Amanda said encouragingly. "Yes, that's a good idea. My Dad has some tools you could use, I'm sure he wouldn't mind if we borrowed them."

Skelly dried his eyes with the back of his hand and smiled at her.

"That's very kind of you," he said, "but there is one slight problem... Ted took my space-egg away and hid it just in case someone discovered it, and I don't know where he has hidden it. On top of all that, I don't know where Ted has moved to or even if he is still alive – I could be marooned here forever."

"How terrible," Amanda remarked. "But why did you come here in the first place anyway?"

"It was a mistake really. You see, my family moved to a new home just as yours did and I felt sad and lonely because I missed my friends, so I decided to run away from home and find them. Therefore, I stepped into my space-egg and travelled into the air but my capsule got caught in the slipstream of a meteor shower which sucked me out of orbit. The rest is history."

Tears welled up in Amanda's eyes.

"What an awfully sad story," she said. "I will never run away from home after hearing that."

Skelly threw his hands into the air in a couldn't-care-less kind of way.

"Well, at least it's been a learning experience," he said with a laugh, trying hard to put on a brave face.

"Yes... really! I'll bet you've got a tale or two to tell though," said Amanda.

"Oh, indeed I have. I've got quite a few, in fact. Would you like to hear one of them?"

"I'd love to," Amanda replied.

"Okay then, let me think for a moment. Oh, yes – here's a good one..."

Then Skelly started chuckling to himself before clearing his throat and eventually commencing the story.

"One day I was down at Farmer Smith's, helping myself to milk from his parlour because I desperately needed a milk fix..."

"You're obviously addicted to milk then?" Amanda said questioningly.

"Whereas a human's body is made up from a large percentage of water, our bodies on Laktose are made up from milk," Skelly explained, "therefore, milk is necessary for my survival because it is the life-force for the people of my planet."

"I see," said Amanda. "Sorry to interrupt."

"That's quite alright," said Skelly, and he continued his conversation where he had left off. "Anyway, the old farmer had a dairy farm and I thought he wouldn't miss a little drop of milk. Well, I was busy helping myself when Farmer Smith walked into the milking parlour. Luckily, he didn't see me, but I had to get out of sight before he did and the only place I could find to hide was in a milk churn. As my luck goes it was three-quarters full of milk and then, to cap it all, Farmer Smith walked over and put the lid on the churn!"

"Oh my goodness," said Amanda, stifling a laugh.

"It gets worse," Skelly told her. "The next thing he did was to pick up the milk churn and put it on the back of his pick-up truck to take to market. But, as he drove around a sharp bend in the road, Farmer Smith collided with a bus that was travelling in the opposite direction and the force of our impact caused the churn to roll off the truck and burst open. Mind you, it was a good thing really because it was cold, wet and dark inside the milk churn and I desperately needed to get out. I shall never forget the look of horror on the passengers' faces afterwards when I stopped beside the bus, shivering and covered in frothy white stuff, to pull faces at all of them before taking off across the fields as quick as my legs would take me."

Amanda was in fits of laughter by now.

"That's such a funny story," she said between giggles. "You must have looked quite a sight. I'll bet the passengers all thought they had seen a ghost!"

"Well, it certainly was an unexpected fright for them and it gave them something to talk about for a long time afterwards," Skelly agreed.

At that moment, a loud voice – that sounded as if it came from nearby – interrupted their conversation.

"Where are you Amanda? It's time to come in now and get ready for bed," yelled her mother.

"I'm on my way Mum," Amanda shouted her reply, trying hard not to give away her location.

"I'll be back as soon as I possibly can," Amanda told Skelly as she stood up ready to depart. "It's really nice to meet you and, don't worry, I'll be your friend and I won't tell anyone about you either."

With that, she left the barn and went to find her mother.

"I hope you haven't been playing in that old barn," Mum said, rather sternly, when she entered the house.

Amanda knew that she was not allowed inside the barn and she hated lying because it was a really bad trait but, when she gave this some thought, she realised that she had actually been talking in the barn and not playing, so she did not consider her forthcoming answer to be a lie.

"No I haven't been playing in the barn," she said.

"Good, because I've already warned you that it is not safe. Not only that, but you don't know what you might find in there," said

Mum. "It's nearly dark now, so go and get ready for bed; your dad will tuck in your covers very shortly."

Half-an-hour later Amanda's father came into her bedroom to wish her goodnight, whereupon he found that she had been eagerly waiting to ask him a question.

"Whereabouts is the Milky Way, Dad?" she asked.

"What an extraordinary question for you to ask," said Dad. "You've never shown an interest in the stars before, so where did that one come from?"

"Oh, it was just some place that a friend of mine told me all about," replied Amanda, "and I was just wondering where it was."

Her father walked over to the window, where he pulled back the curtains and peered through the glass. It was a clear night and the moon and stars shone brightly against their dark backdrop.

"I'll show you the Milky Way," said Dad. "Come over here and take a look."

He lifted up his daughter so that she was sitting on the windowsill, and then he pointed a finger in the direction of a long band of pale white that spread thinly across the night sky.

"That light-coloured plume is the Milky Way," he explained. "It's a galaxy made up of a huge cluster of stars. There are millions of them – possibly billions or trillions – but nobody knows for sure."

"Wow! That's amazing. You know everything, right Dad?"

"Far from it… Yes, there are certain subjects of which I do have a certain amount of knowledge – and that includes astronomy – but I don't know everything."

"What's astronomy Dad?"

"It is the scientific study of celestial bodies such as planets or stars."

"Well, if you know something about planets and things, would you know which of those stars is called Laktose?"

"I've never even heard of it," said Dad.

"It's a sweet little planet apparently," Amanda said in all innocence.

Dad roared with laughter upon hearing this.

"I think someone is having you on," he said. "I've heard of lactose, which is a sugar found in milk, but I've never heard of a star with a similar sounding name. When I get the time I may well look that one up to see what I can find out about it. Come along now – into bed young lady, it's time you were asleep."

Amanda's father kissed her goodnight and left the bedroom. She was pleased that she had found a new friend to talk to and she lay awake for a while wondering what Skelly's home planet was really like. When she eventually nodded off to sleep she dreamt about the planet Laktose and that Skelly would soon be able to return home to be reunited with his family and friends.

CHAPTER FOUR

The Milk Bandit

One weekday morning Mum walked into the kitchen with a perplexed look on her face. As she entered the room Dad glanced up from his newspaper and caught sight of her pained expression.

"What's the matter dear?" he asked.

"The milkman has left an extra pint of milk today and I didn't ask him to," she explained. "I shall have to have a word with him when he comes to collect the milk money next Saturday because nothing seems to make any sense – one day he doesn't leave enough milk and then on another day he leaves too many bottles – It's most odd! I don't know what is going on but I will find out."

"Hmm," grunted her husband in agreement, and he buried his head in the newspaper again.

"I expect he's a typical country bumpkin – and illiterate as well – I'll bet that he can't even read the notes I leave for him and he just guesses what they say," Mum continued to rant.

"Yes dear," replied her husband, but this time without even bothering to glance upwards.

Amanda sniggered out loud. She had sat quietly eating her breakfast until this point whilst listening to her mother's complaining.

"What's so funny Amanda?" she asked, scowling at her.

"I think the whole thing is funny," Amanda replied. "I mean, after all, does it really matter if we've got too much milk one day and not enough on another, just as long as it evens out?"

"Yes, it does matter," snapped her mother. "It's the principle of the whole thing. I'm the one who has to pay the bill and, who knows, maybe the milkman is trying to rip me off and get money for nothing. Now hurry up and eat your breakfast or you will be late for school."

Amanda did exactly as she was told. She could see that her mother was not in a very good mood that morning, and she knew that it would be no use starting an argument because it would mean that she would probably find herself grounded and then she would not be able to pay a visit to Skelly.

When the following Saturday came around Amanda and her father were watching a film in the sitting room after lunch when there was a knock at the door.

"I'll get that," came Mum's voice from the kitchen. "It's probably the milkman."

She was right, it was the milkman. He was a jovial-looking fellow with a ruddy complexion, who beamed warmly at her when she opened the door, showing off a set of pure white teeth.

"Mornin' Mrs James," said the milkman. "Oi'm Dave. It's nice to meet you. Have you and your family settled in yet?"

Then he held his hand out towards Amanda's mother in a polite gesture. She shook hands with the man rather reluctantly because she was a bit of a snob about touching people she had never met. Not only that, but she was quite taken aback by the man's warm manner because she had actually opened the door with the intention of tearing the milkman off a strip or two.

"Oi've come to collect me milk money," said Dave in his broad West Country accent.

"Yes, I was expecting you this morning," Mum replied rather abruptly.

"It's a big round Oi 'ave and it takes time to..." began Dave, but he was cut short.

"Can I have the bill please?"

"Oh, okay... Oi don't usually give out a bill though, 'cause people round 'ere trusts me, but if you really want a bill you can 'ave this one in me book," Dave obligingly agreed.

He tore the page from his sales ledger and handed it to Amanda's mum who had been staring open-mouthed as she listened, somewhat in awe of his country dialect.

"I'll go and get me... er... I mean, *my* purse," she said. "I'll be back in just a moment."

Mum took the bill into her kitchen and checked the amounts against the daily list that she had kept. To her surprise, it was correct in every detail. She returned to the hallway and handed Dave the money, with a look of surprise still showing upon her face.

"Is something wrong?" enquired Dave.

"Not really... Well, yes, as a matter of fact there is something wrong!" Mum replied. "Sometimes you give me an extra bottle of milk when I don't even order it and then on other days I am a pint short... Is there any particular reason how this can possibly happen?"

Dave removed his flat cap, smoothed down the few strands of hair that grew on top of his bright pink scalp, and scratched his head as he puzzled over this.

"Oi always leaves what you asks for," he said. "It's usually two pints a day unless you puts a note for more or less."

"Yes, but it doesn't always happen like that," said Mum rather scornfully.

All of a sudden, Dave began to laugh because it had dawned on him what was going on.

"Oh, it's only the Milk Bandit!" he exclaimed knowingly, placing his cap back onto his head.

"*The Milk Bandit!* – Who on Earth is The Milk Bandit?" gasped Mum.

"Oi can tell you're from outta town, 'cause you never would 'ave 'eard of him would you? Let me explain... Y'see, somebody round 'ere steals the milk from the doorsteps and on other occasions they puts it back, so we calls 'em the Milk Bandit," Dave informed her.

"Don't the police do anything about it?" asked Mum, who was feeling quite stunned by this revelation.

Dave laughed again.

"No," he said. "It's been goin' on for years now and everyone's used to it. Even the local bobby loses his milk some days and then on another day 'e gains some. Nobody bothers complaining 'cause it 'as an 'abit of working out so that no-one loses at the end of the day. Oi know it must sound strange to you but we've learned to live with it."

"Well, I don't know if I ever will," retorted Mum.

"Oh, you'll get used to it – believe me, everyone does."

"Does anyone have any idea who this so-called Milk Bandit is?" asked Mum.

"No. People 'as guesses but nobody's really sure. Some say that it's a ghost 'cause many years ago a load of people on a bus 'appened to see one float away from an upturned milk churn. Oi once believed that too 'cause Oi was on that same bus, but Oi was just a boy then an' didn't know any different."

Amanda had been listening to the whole conversation from the living room doorway and she burst into hysterical laughter at this remark, for she now knew exactly who the Milk Bandit was. Upon hearing this, her mother turned around and glared at her, so she quickly darted away to disappear back into the living room.

"I really don't know what to make of all this," said Mum. "A Milk Bandit who turns out to be a ghost! It's the most extraordinary story I've ever heard."

"Well, that's what folks believe 'round 'ere, so we just accepts it," said Dave. "Now, if you'll excuse me, Oi best be on me way 'cause Oi've got a lot to do today."

"Yes, I expect you 'ave... I mean, *have*... er, thank you for enlightening me Dave."

"That's quite alright Mrs James," said Dave, tilting his cap politely. "If there's ever anything yer needs to know just ask me or the postmaster 'cause we know most things around 'ere. G'day now."

"Yes I'm sure you do," muttered Mum as she watched Dave walk back to his old-fashioned, three-wheeled milk float. Then she closed the front door and walked into the living room to relate the story to her husband.

"I have to agree that the ghost story is most odd," he said, "but the main thing is, if there are no discrepancies in the bill then I wouldn't worry too much about it."

"That's not the point," replied his wife. "I'm beginning to wonder what manner of place we've moved to. You would never have heard such ridiculous nonsense in the city."

"That's the beauty of living in the country my dear," Dad said with a sigh. "Nothing much happens in rural places so people need to brighten up their lives. The story you've just heard is probably simple country folklore."

Mum rounded on Amanda next.

"I think that was very rude of you to eavesdrop, Amanda; and I didn't find the man's story to be at all funny... Theft is a serious matter you know!"

"Oh, Mum... but it is a funny story. Imagine, a ghost running around stealing milk from people's doorsteps! And he doesn't do any serious harm either."

Her mother was spoiling for an argument and she opened her mouth to bawl at Amanda, but her father saw this coming so he quickly came to Amanda's aid before anything could be said.

"Yes, you have to admit that it is quite amusing," he agreed.

Mum threw her arms in the air in despair.

"Huh, I give up! You're both as bad as one another," she snorted. "But I'll show you. I'll catch the little blighter – this so-called Milk Bandit – then we'll see who's laughing."

In the next instance Amanda and her father watched Mum storm out of the kitchen.

"Watch out!" said Dad, after she had gone. "Your mum is on the warpath again and she means business. Woe betide us all, especially the poor old Milk Bandit."

Amanda's father always did see the funny side of things and this made her chuckle.

"While your mum has this bee in her bonnet I think we'd better make ourselves scarce," Dad continued. "I've got to go into town and buy some bits and pieces; do you want to come along with me?

We can even find somewhere to have a burger or pizza if you'd like to."

"Yeah, yeah, yeah!" said Amanda, jumping for joy. "Come on, let's go."

She had not been taken out for a burger since they had moved to the village because the nearest large town with a fast-food outlet was quite some distance away now; therefore, just the thought of this notion made her mouth water.

It was late in the evening when Amanda and her father returned home from town and they were greeted by a most unusual sight, because Mum was perched rather precariously on the top rung of a stepladder, erecting a strange-looking tarpaulin over the front porch, which turned out to be a military camouflage net. She stopped what she was doing when she saw them and grinned triumphantly at both of them as they approached her with their mouths agape.

"What in Heaven's name are you up to now?" gasped Dad.

Mum climbed down from the stepladder and stood with her hands on her hips as she admired her handiwork.

"What do you think?" she said smugly. "That ought to do the trick."

"What trick exactly?" asked her husband.

"Well, when the supposed Milk Bandit comes to steal my milk, then this tripwire will trigger the net to fall and capture the villain. I don't know why anybody hasn't thought of it before," she exclaimed proudly. "It obviously takes someone with an ounce of intelligence to move into the village and come up with the idea."

"Yes dear!" Dad said rather patronisingly as he stared at the Heath-Robinson type affair that his wife had rigged-up. Then he shook his head despairingly and turned away to enter the house, whereupon Amanda followed him.

"It's worse than I thought," Dad told her when they were safely out of earshot. "I think your mother has completely lost her marbles this time!"

"I guess the best thing for us to do is to humour her then," remarked Amanda.

"I thought that was what we usually did," joked her father. "Well, if it makes her happy, let her get on with it and let's hope that she doesn't become too obsessed with her quest... You know what she can be like."

Amanda agreed with him and then she changed the subject.

"Please can I go outside to play again, Dad?" she asked.

"Yes, go and have some fun," he replied, "before you are too old, and married to a lunatic like I am. Oh, woe is me!"

Dad walked away, chuckling to himself and, once Amanda was outside, she immediately went to the barn in order to find Skelly and warn him about the trap that her mother had set.

"It's not the first time anyone has tried to capture me," he said, merely laughing at the idea, "and I'm sure it won't be the last."

"Yes, I'm sure it won't be the last time either," Amanda worriedly replied. "You don't know my mum!"

"Let me tell you a little tale," said Skelly. "There was once a horrible old man called Mr Barnett, who used to live here in the village, and I regularly borrowed milk from his doorstep because he was so mean. One morning he tried to catch me out by replacing the milk in the bottles with a white coloured liquid, expecting me to drink it, but as soon as I set eyes on it I could tell that something wasn't quite right. I took the silver top off one of the bottles and sniffed at it but it didn't smell like milk does, so I put the foil lid loosely on the bottle and took it away with me to examine it. The stuff in the bottles turned out to be Milk of Magnesia – which is a form of laxative – which he had left out for me in the belief that I would drink it and become quite ill."

"How awful," Amanda interrupted "What a nasty man."

"Yes, but I turned the tables on him," said Skelly, winking at her. "You see, I added some flour and water to the liquid to give it a thicker texture so that it actually resembled milk, and then, the next morning, I returned to his house where I hid in some bushes waiting for young Dave the milkman to arrive. After he had been and gone I swapped the bottles of mixture for the real milk – and very tasty it was too. Of course, Mr Barnett was a bit stupid and I knew that he was bound to drink the liquid because he wouldn't be able to tell the difference."

"I don't think you should have done that," Amanda told him. "You might have done him some serious harm."

"Oh no, I knew it wouldn't have done him any serious harm… Anyway, he was going to do the same to me, wasn't he?"

"I guess so, but two wrongs don't make a right," she said. "What happened next?"

"I peered through his kitchen window, watching him as he poured the liquid onto his breakfast cereal and then gobbled it all up, and I couldn't believe it when the greedy pig decided to have a second large helping of cereal. Well, a short while later he ran with some haste to the toilet because the laxative was beginning to take effect, and while he was in there I sneaked into his house to pour the rest of the disgusting liquid away and replace it with real milk so that he didn't drink any more of it. After that, Mr Barnett spent the rest of the day running in and out of the bathroom – and it jolly well served him right too."

"So you gave him a taste of his own medicine, so to speak," laughed Amanda.

"Yes, he never ever set a trap for me again."

Amanda suddenly had a frightful thought.

"You wouldn't do such a thing to us, would you Skelly?" she asked rather worriedly.

"Oh, Heavens, no! Mr Barnett deserved it because he was such a horrid old man but your family are exactly the opposite because you are nice people. I know that your mum doesn't really mean to do me any harm – she's only trying to catch the Milk Bandit because it would give her a feeling of great satisfaction."

"I am glad that you wouldn't harm us," said a relieved Amanda, and then she changed the subject. "Unfortunately, I have to go now Skelly because my parents will be wondering where I am. I shall come back and see you as soon as I possibly can though."

"I understand. Thanks for warning me about the trap," replied Skelly as Amanda left the old barn.

Nobody in the James household was allowed to use the front door thenceforth, because Mum was afraid that someone would set off the trap she had laid. This was a major inconvenience at first; however, it was not to last for very long because, just after dawn had broken on the following Monday morning, Amanda awoke with a start when she heard an awful din going on outside the house. It took a few seconds for her to open her sleepy eyes and come to, but then she suddenly remembered her mother's trap. At the same time, she could hear Mum calling out for someone to help her; so, as fast as she possibly could, Amanda donned her dressing gown and slippers before racing down the stairs to arrive in the porch at exactly the same moment as her father – who had hurriedly thrown on his bath robe and was wearing only one of his slippers! Here, they beheld an amazing sight, for there on the doorstep was the collapsed camouflage net with Amanda's mum lying spread-eagle on top of it, trying to pin down the struggling bundle beneath her.

"I've caught the Milk Bandit! I've caught the Milk Bandit!" she screeched. "Quick Bill, help me turn it over and we can find out who it is."

But, as her husband stretched forward at his wife's request for help, a vaguely familiar voice reached their ears.

"What's 'appening to me missus?" it said.

Upon hearing this, Mum froze and glanced up, at which point she espied Dave's milk float at the end of the driveway and a look of horror spread across her face. When she looked down again her husband had already pulled back a portion of the camouflage net to reveal the face of the Milk Bandit, and she found herself staring directly into the ruddy and somewhat startled features of Dave the milkman!

Having been concerned until now that Skelly had actually been captured by her mother, Amanda immediately let out a huge sigh of relief before bursting into fits of giggles as the whole charade instantly became clear to her. It seemed that poor Dave had been going about his daily routine when he had become the innocent victim of her mother's ridiculous plan to capture the Milk Bandit.

Apologetically, and rather sheepishly, Amanda's parents helped Dave to his feet and removed the net that had engulfed the bewildered milkman. Dad placed his hands over his eyes, feeling quite embarrassed about his wife's foolish antics and not at all wanting to be associated with it, whilst Mum frantically tried to smooth the creases from the dishevelled-looking milkman's clothes.

When she had finished doing this, Dave stretched his aching limbs and then nervously combed down the few strands of hair on his head with his fingers, at the same time looking around for his flat cap that had become dislodged in the tussle. Still giggling, Amanda picked up the cap from the ground and she handed it to the poor milkman, incapable of saying a single word.

"I'm s-s-so s-s-sorry," Mum stammered.

"We're both sorry," added Dad.

"It was a trap you s-s-see... f-f-for the Milk Bandit," Mum went on.

Dave the milkman looked at Amanda's mother as if he felt pity because she had not caught the Milk Bandit after all.

"There's no need to apologise," he said. "It's no bother 'cause Oi understands what yer was trying to do."

And, in that same instance, his face cracked up as he began to grin incessantly.

"Well, no 'arm done," he chortled.

"W-would you like a cup of tea?" Mum tried to insist.

"No thanks m'love," he said. "Gorra lot to do today. G'day to y'all."

With that, he adjusted his cap and strode back to his milk float, whistling merrily away to himself as if nothing had happened.

Dad stared enquiringly at his wife for a moment or two, trying hard to restrain a laugh, and then he looked at Amanda before addressing the pair of them.

"I shall eat my own words after saying nothing exciting ever happens in country life," he spluttered. "In fact, the way things are looking, I would say that at least Amanda and I are going to find it very interesting – if not amusing – living here."

His wife glowered at him, grunted something unrepeatable and then she stormed away in disgust, leaving Amanda and her father to collapse in a heap with uncontrollable hysterics.

CHAPTER FIVE

Skelly Becomes Homeless

During the next few days Amanda learned from Skelly that he possessed some quite extraordinary powers and, on one particular visit to the run-down barn, she was treated to a close glimpse of nature that she would never have witnessed without his help.

"I would like to show you something," Skelly said to Amanda one evening. "Are you afraid of heights?"

"I don't know," replied the girl. "I climbed a tree once and that didn't frighten me, although it wasn't really much taller than me."

"Up there, on the rafters," said Skelly as he pointed towards the roof, "live a family of barn owls – or screech owls as they are sometimes known – and the mother owl has just hatched some fledglings. Would you like to see them?"

"I've never seen an owl, let alone a barn owl, so that would be really nice," Amanda told him. "But how do we get up there?"

If you climb onto my back and hold on tight I will lift you up."

Amanda stared at Skelly in disbelief. She was a lot taller than he was and she could not see how she was going to be able to gain any extra height by climbing onto his back. However, Skelly seemed to realise what Amanda was thinking.

"Trust me," he said with a grin, "and do make sure that you have a firm grip on me."

Feeling rather awkward, Amanda did what Skelly asked of her, although he was so much smaller than Amanda and she had to bend down to get onto her tiny friend's back. Suddenly, at the very moment that she climbed aboard, Skelly's limbs began to stretch at a fantastic rate until they were ten times their normal length. His extra-long arms then reached upwards to grasp the ledge high above them and slowly, but steadily, the duo rose up towards the eaves. Amanda clung on for dear life as she glanced over her shoulder at the ground that was being left far beneath them, whereupon she noticed that Skelly's legs were now stretched to many times their normal length also.

They eventually stopped rising when they reached the eaves of the old barn, where Amanda peered over Skelly's shoulder to gaze at the family of owls in pure delight. Three baby owls sat in their nest with their beaks wide open while their father fed them regurgitated food that he had caught on his early evening flight. Meanwhile, their broody mother sat upon another egg, patiently waiting for it to hatch. Skelly and Amanda were then treated to a rare experience for, as they quietly observed, there was a light tapping sound and a hairline crack appeared in the egg right before their very eyes. Following this, the eggshell broke into two pieces and the newly hatched owl chick began to wriggle about as it took its first few gulps of fresh air.

Throughout the whole spectacle the pair remained silent so that they did not disturb the owls and, after the chick had hatched, they watched for a further few moments before Skelly nodded to Amanda that they were about to return to ground level. Within seconds they were safely back on the floor of the barn as Skelly's limbs shrunk back to their normal size.

"Wow! That was amazing," gasped an awestruck Amanda.

"Thank you so much Skelly. I feel so lucky to have been able to see the owls because I am sure that many people do not see such a beautiful thing in their entire lifetime, and I am only nine years old."

"I thought that you would enjoy it," said Skelly with a massive grin on his face, because he was pleased to have given Amanda such enormous pleasure.

"Not only that, but the whole stretching thing... What an experience! How did you manage to do it?"

"Well, it's no big deal for me really because we inhabitants of the Milky Way have a body mass that is mainly made up from milk. Therefore, the amount of calcium in our bodies make our bones really supple, which – when coupled with the molecular structure of our jelly-like flesh – enable us to mould our form into all sorts of shapes."

"Really? All sorts of shapes?"

"As long as it is a relatively flexible item," replied Skelly. "Given time, I am sure that you will get to see some of these shapes that I can become."

"I can't wait to see," said Amanda, but her excitement rapidly began to wane when, in the next second, she glanced at her watch.

"Oh dear, is that the time?" she said. "It goes by so quickly when you are having fun. I really must rush away before I get into serious trouble. Bye for now Skelly – see you soon."

The young girl ran home, desperately wishing that she could tell somebody about her new experiences, but she realised that there was not a soul she could tell, apart from Tabs the cat. Although Tabs normally stared nonchalantly into space when Amanda spoke to her, sometimes the cat did not even bother to open her eyes at all, but Amanda believed that she was really taking in the information that was being fed to her and when she was out gallivanting in her own little cat community Tabs surely related Amanda's exciting stories.

Every day the school bus stopped at the end of Amanda's driveway in order to drop her off, and one sunny weekday afternoon Amanda stepped off the bus to saunter casually along the drive. Lazily kicking pieces of gravel as she walked, her mind was far away whilst deep in thought about a party that she had been invited to during the coming weekend. In her dreamy state, Amanda closed her eyes and threw back her head, soaking up the warm rays of afternoon sunshine, but when she opened her eyes again she could not believe what she saw. Immediately dropping her school bags onto the gravel, she ran across the lawn as fast as her legs would carry her.

It appeared that work had already started on the barn without her knowledge, for there was a pick-up truck parked in the turning area in front of the house, complete with ladders and wheelbarrows and all those tools that builders use in their trade. Not only that, but Amanda could see the builders hard at work stripping the old tiles from the barn roof.

"Where will the owls live now?" was Amanda's first thought as she ran hard, and then another terrible thought came into her head.

"Oh no!" she said out loud. "Poor Skelly will be made homeless too – Whatever will become of him?"

Amanda ran even harder now, with these thoughts spinning around in her head like a whirlpool. She had also spotted smoke rising into the air behind the barn and, when she reached the far corner of the old building, there she saw her father sorting out the contents that had littered the barn's interior for so many years, and he was throwing them onto a bonfire. On the lawn in front of him was the battered suitcase that Skelly always slept in, and Dad was about to impale it with a garden fork before tossing it onto the fire.

Amanda screamed at the top of her voice to try and get his attention, but it was too late because her father was already in the motion of swinging the fork towards the large suitcase. Then he pierced it with all four prongs, which made Amanda's screams turn to hysteria.

The men who were working on the roof immediately stopped what they were doing to see what the commotion was all about, whilst Amanda's father froze on the spot, clinging tightly to the garden fork that now supported the skewered luggage case in a mid-air position.

"Whatever is the matter with you Amanda?" asked Dad, with an extremely worried look on his face.

"*He's in there! He's in there!*" she shrieked.

Dad stared at the suitcase, lowered it to the ground and quickly withdrew the garden fork before casting it to one side. In a mad panic he threw open the lid, only to find that it was completely empty. Having seen this, Amanda collapsed on the lawn in a heap; partly through exhaustion at having run so fast and partly from the relief of knowing that Skelly was not in the suitcase after all.

"What do you mean, '*he's in there*?' Who's in where?" asked Dad in a somewhat confused state.

Amanda had to think fast.

"Er… The owls are in the barn," she jabbered, pointing excitedly towards the building.

"I don't know why you are making such a big fuss about it. We already know that the owls are in there!" he snapped. "Don't worry about them, they will be fine… we're working around them."

Then Dad placed his hands on his hips and appeared to look rather annoyed.

"Strewth Amanda, you frightened the life out of me. For a moment or two I thought there was someone in the suitcase, judging by the way you were screaming your head off!"

Amanda tried to make out that this was funny and she giggled pathetically. At that moment her mother appeared on the scene, also out of breath because she had run across the lawn from the house after hearing Amanda's pitiful screaming.

"What's the matter with Amanda?" she yelled in panic as she bent down and began to inspect her daughter from top to bottom, pulling her first one way and then the other.

"There's absolutely nothing wrong with her at all," retorted her husband. "She was worried about the owls in the barn, would you believe!"

The anxious look on her mother's face rapidly vanished, only to be replaced with an angry scowl. Then she stood up and towered over Amanda, shaking her finger violently in her direction.

"How do you know there are owls in the barn?" she asked.

But Amanda did not have to answer because Mum had already drawn her own conclusion.

"Well," she continued. "I would say that the only way you could possibly have known about them was by going inside the building when I distinctly told you to keep out. I will not have disobedience in this household – Go to your room this instance!"

Amanda tried to argue, although in vain.

"But Mum…" she began.

"But Mum nothing! Do as you're told, and don't leave your room until I tell you."

Without any hesitation whatsoever, Amanda picked herself up from the lawn and ran to the house before her mother lost her temper altogether and slapped her.

"Phew, that was close," muttered Amanda once she was safely indoors, but then she forgot all about her reprimand as her mind turned to other thoughts.

"If Skelly wasn't in the suitcase or in the barn, then where was he?" she asked herself.

For the next hour Amanda lay on her bed wondering what had happened to her little friend. Then she heard the builders drive away in their van. After that a further hour passed by, during which time she watched the sun move closer to the horizon, and all the while a faint snoring sound reached her ears, although it had not fully registered in her head until now. Tabs often snored in her sleep so this was nothing new, but it suddenly dawned on her that Tabs was purring too.

"Snoring and purring at the same time? That just couldn't be possible," Amanda said, thinking out loud.

Instantly on the alert, she sat up on her bed and listened carefully as she tried to pinpoint exactly where the snoring sound was coming from. After hunting high and low all around the bedroom, she eventually discovered that the sound was coming from the top of her wardrobe. To be absolutely sure, Amanda pulled her bedroom chair in front of the wardrobe and climbed onto it, which enabled her to be just about capable of peering over the top of the wardrobe when she stood on tiptoes. Sure enough, once she had done this, her suspicions were confirmed for there she found Skelly, curled up sound asleep and clutching her favourite teddy bear close to his chest. It seemed a shame to have to wake him but Amanda knew that if she could hear him snoring then so too would her parents if they came into her bedroom. So, she shook Skelly hard and he awoke with a start, almost falling headfirst off the wardrobe.

"What's the matter?" he asked, rubbing his sleepy eyes. "Why did you wake me up?"

"You can't stay in here," whispered Amanda, "because someone will find you."

"The builders are demolishing my home," said a frightened little voice. "Where will I live now?"

"I don't know, let me think for a moment," replied Amanda, and then she had a brainwave. "You told me that you can change shape; in that case, could you change into an inanimate object of some sort so that you blend in with the surroundings?"

"Such as what?" asked Skelly.

"Such as..." said Amanda as she hurriedly looked around her bedroom, "... such as a new backpack for instance."

For a couple of seconds Skelly studied Amanda's own backpack that was propped up beneath the window. It had been manufactured in the shape of a frog and he decided to try to copy it. All of a sudden he began to quiver, which was combined with a strange popping sound, and within moments a replica frog backpack magically appeared to replace him. A thoroughly delighted Amanda placed her hands on her cheeks and chuckled merrily away to herself.

"That's fantastic," she squealed, "but there's only one problem... frogs aren't usually white! How about changing into a polar bear shape instead?"

Of its own accord, the backpack began to quiver and pop just like before and, in place of it, there suddenly appeared a cute little polar bear.

"Or maybe a floppy white bunny," came the next suggestion.

At her request, the backpack obligingly changed shape once more and Amanda continued to giggle in delight.

"Wow! This is fun," she chuckled. "Now I can have any backpack I want without having to pay for it. I could even have a different one for every day of the week. Hey! Now there's a thought... I could put my books into the backpack and take you to school with me. How do you like that idea Skelly?"

Upon hearing this, Skelly changed back to his usual shape.

"That sounds like fun," he said. "I've never been to school."

Before Amanda could draw breath to add her next remark their conversation was interrupted by the sound of creaking wooden floorboards as someone began to climb the stairs.

"Quick, disguise yourself as a floppy white bunny," whispered Amanda, "...and hurry!"

Luckily, Skelly had only just managed to change shape when Dad entered the bedroom.

"Who are you talking to?" he asked, glancing all around him at the same time, half expecting to find someone else in the room with her.

"Nobody; I was talking to myself," Amanda guiltily replied, and she felt a surge of blood rush to her cheeks when she began to blush.

"Your mother says you can come downstairs for supper and then it will be early to bed for you tonight," Dad told her. "And, for goodness sake, don't say anything that will upset your mum or you'll be in deep trouble with her."

After finishing his sentence he took a step forwards, tripped over the rabbit backpack that was lying in the middle of the bedroom floor and almost fell flat on his face. Rather annoyed by this, Dad composed himself, picked up the backpack and examined it from top to bottom.

"I haven't seen this before," he said. "It's made of a weird kind of material that feels a bit like jelly – how bizarre!"

Mumbling away to himself as he studied it, he soon lost interest in the backpack and flung it with some force onto Amanda's bedroom chair.

"I could have broken my neck falling over that thing," Dad complained. "Do try to keep your bedroom tidy Amanda – it looks as if a bomb has hit it!"

With that, her father turned around and left the bedroom.

"Ouch! That really hurt," moaned Skelly in a nasally voice, for his nose had become squashed against the back of the chair when he landed. "I could have broken my neck too you know."

"Sssh!" Amanda whispered. "You'll be found out if you don't keep quiet."

She picked up the backpack and turned it around before placing Skelly upright on the chair so that he would be in a more comfortable position.

"There, that's better isn't it?" she said. "Now, don't move from that spot – I'll be back later."

Amanda then left the bedroom and went downstairs to join her parents for supper.

CHAPTER SIX

Skelly Goes to School

Amanda awoke at dawn the next morning, as soon as the birds began to sing. Feeling quite refreshed after her enforced early night, she leapt from her bed and pulled back her bedroom curtains to reveal another bright, sunny day. Having spent the night in the shape of a floppy rabbit, Skelly had since reverted to his normal form and he was sat upon Amanda's bedroom chair with his arms folded and his legs crossed, whilst an unhappy frown showed upon his face.

"What's the matter?" asked Amanda.

Skelly parted his pouting lips to grumble his reply.

"I didn't have a very good night's sleep," he complained. "What, with you and Tabs snoring, it sounded as if someone was sawing timber in here all night long!"

"I'm sorry," Amanda apologised, "but when we're asleep none of us have any control over what we do – and that includes you too. Yesterday you were snoring in your sleep also."

Skelly ignored Amanda's apology.

"Well, I hope it's not going to be like that every night because I will have to find somewhere else to sleep if that's the case," he grumpily retorted.

Amanda could tell that Skelly was not in the best of moods that morning.

"I see! Got out of bed on the wrong side have you?" she snapped.

"Well, if you're in such a bad mood, then maybe it's not a good idea to take you to school with me today. Heaven knows what could happen."

Upon hearing this remark, Skelly's frown miraculously disappeared and he suddenly gave the appearance of being much more cheerful.

"Oh no, I don't want to stay here on my own. I'm really looking forward to going to school with you today. Please take me with you Amanda," he said, fluttering his eyelashes at her.

Amanda could not help but smile for she found it difficult to stay angry with Skelly for long, especially when he gave her his 'butter-might-melt-in-your-mouth' look.

"Very well then, I will take you to school but only if you promise not to be miserable," she surrendered.

"I promise," said Skelly, a big cheesy grin suddenly appearing on his face.

"Now that we've managed to sort that matter out I must go and get ready for school, and then I shall collect you after breakfast," said Amanda. "Do you need a drink of milk?"

"Oh, my goodness! Yes, of course I do. In the heat of the moment I very nearly forgot. It wouldn't do for your new backpack to change colour in the middle of the day, would it? That really would take some explaining."

"I'll bring you a glass of milk after my breakfast," Amanda told him. "For the time being though, you really must change back into a floppy rabbit shape, just in case Mum or Dad walk into the room."

Proudly sporting her new backpack, Amanda stood at the foot of her driveway waiting for the school bus to collect her. As usual, the bus arrived on time and she boarded it; after which, there were many comments from her friends as she walked along the centre aisle and climbed the stairs to the upper deck.

"Oh, that's so adorable," exclaimed Clare.

"What a cute rabbit," said Vicky.

"Yes, where did you get it? I want one," Jenny added.

"It belongs to my friend and I'm only borrowing it," Amanda replied, hoping that her friends would not question her too deeply. She did not like to tell lies because her face would turn bright red and would give the game away. Luckily for her, nobody persevered with the subject of where she had obtained her new backpack.

Throughout the entire journey to school Skelly kept his eyes wide open, allowing himself to become totally absorbed with taking in his new surroundings. Although he could not allow his eyes to blink, for fear of giving his identity away, he could still roll them around so that he could get full vision all about him. He noticed that there were lots of children on the bus and they were so noisy he wished that he could stick his fingers in his ears to deaden the sound. And when he arrived at Amanda's school he could not believe his eyes because never before had he seen so many children all in one place, milling around like busy little insects.

Shortly after their arrival at the school a loud clanging sound almost made Skelly jump out of his jelly-like skin – which turned out to be the school bell that always announced the start of lessons for the day – and in a disorderly fashion the children shuffled into their classrooms.

In Amanda's classroom the desks were arranged into three rows, where the pupils sat side by side in each row because they sometimes had to share school textbooks. Amanda's desk was situated on the left-hand side of the centre row, precisely halfway down the classroom. She sat down next to Clare, her friend who was on the bus – they always sat together – and Amanda placed her backpack at her feet underneath her desk. Meanwhile, the form teacher – Miss Anne Throwpee – watched the unruly throng like a hawk as they entered the classroom.

"Settle down now," she boomed in a stern voice.

At the sound of her no-nonsense monotones the burble of excited chatter petered out, to be replaced with absolute silence.

"Good morning children," rumbled Miss Throwpee.

"Good morning Miss," came the compulsory chorus.

Miss Throwpee stared at the children disdainfully. She was quite a formidable-looking woman with an old-fashioned beehive hairstyle and half-moon spectacles that seemed to balance precariously on the edge of her nose and, although the teacher was only about thirty years of age, she looked as if she had been around since time began. Her lack of dress sense did not help her appearance in the slightest for she still wore clothes that could easily have come out of someone's wardrobe from the 1960s. No, Miss Throwpee was not renowned for her good taste at all, but she was a fair woman. She had an abrupt manner – some may even refer to her as a bit of a dragon – and she was not one for mincing words by any stretch of the imagination. However, Amanda liked her.

Miss Throwpee rummaged around in her desk drawers for the next few moments and then, placing her hands on the desk in front of her and squaring back her shoulders, she began to grumble and growl.

"Oh bother! I've forgotten something... Turn to page 23 of your exercise books, children – I'll be back in a few ticks."

This was all part of Miss Throwpee's normal routine. Everyone knew that she had not really forgotten anything at all but she was, in fact, going outside to sit in her car to have a crafty smoke of a cigarette, even though smoking was banned on school premises. But Miss Throwpee was a rule unto herself and, throughout the day, she could often be spotted in her car with a cigarette dangling from her elegant cigarette holder that was made from pure amber, whilst pouring over a copy of her favourite monthly magazine entitled *'Life's Natural Disasters'*.

Now, every school has at least one bully and Amanda's school was no exception because directly in front of her sat an extremely obnoxious boy named Terry Bull, who was the classroom bully. As soon as Miss Throwpee had left the room Terry turned around and snatched Amanda's backpack from the floor, which he had set his eyes on from the moment that she had walked into the classroom. Then he sprang from his chair and immediately started chanting out a rhyme in a sing-song sort of fashion:

"Mandy's got a new bag... Mandy's got a new bag..."

She was crestfallen at the loss of her much-prized possession.

"Hey, give me back my backpack," she demanded, "...and... and my name is Amanda not Mandy."

"Same thing," Terry retorted as he ran around the school desks to escape from Amanda who had now given chase.

She was much quicker on her feet than he was but, just as Amanda had caught up with him, Terry threw the backpack to his friend Colin Upstart, who managed to catch it and run off in the opposite direction. Amanda turned around and chased Colin next, who then launched the backpack through the air and returned it to Terry. And so it went on.

Skelly had been taken completely by surprise when he was swept off his feet and he was not quite sure what to make of it all. He could see that Amanda was quite upset at having to play 'Piggy-in-the-Middle' but he was beginning to enjoy the buzz of being thrown through the air.

"Wheee! *Fantazagizmo!*" he squealed to himself as he whistled over Amanda's head, out of reach of her flailing arms. "This is great fun."

But Amanda did not see it that way and she began to sob.

"I want my bag back. Give me back my backpack," she cried.

Naturally, this fell on deaf ears and the two disrespectful boys continued to throw the backpack to each other whilst Amanda tried in vain to retrieve it. Meanwhile, Jack Grimshaw, another accomplice who had been acting as look-out, suddenly ran back to his desk.

"Miss Throwpee's coming back. Quick everyone, sit down," yelled Jack as he plonked himself down on his chair.

The backpack was in mid-flight as Jack gave his warning and Terry made no attempt to catch it. Instead, as the backpack fell to his feet, he lashed out with his foot and kicked it across the room.

"Ouch, that's painful," thought Skelly as Terry's boot landed squarely on his backside, just before he bounced off the blackboard and skidded across the floor to land in a dazed heap in a dusty corner of the classroom.

Amanda was in floods of tears when she picked up poor Skelly from the floor before returning to her desk. By this time the backpack was no longer white. In fact, it was almost stained black from the filthy floor, and Skelly himself was black and blue from his bruises too. Amanda tried to brush him down but she could not remove all of the grime, no matter how hard she tried, so Skelly had to remain a dirty grey colour.

Just as Amanda had sat down, Miss Throwpee re-entered the classroom. The form teacher was astounded by the silence that greeted her, for she was aware that the children would generally misbehave during her absence, and she scoured the room suspiciously to try to find a clue as to what lay behind their quiet expressions. Then Amanda sniffled, which gained Miss Throwpee's immediate attention and caused her to notice that the young girl had been crying.

"What's the matter Amanda?" she asked in a rather concerned voice.

"Nothing Miss," Amanda fibbed.

"Well, people don't usually cry for no apparent reason, so there must be something wrong."

"I'm alright," said Amanda rather adamantly, for she did not want to tell Miss Throwpee about what had really taken place to upset her because it was not the done thing to tell tales on one's classmates.

"Hmmph!" Miss Throwpee snorted disbelievingly.

However, she never failed to miss a trick and she had caught sight of the smirk on Terry Bull's face. He was a known troublemaker and she knew that he was bound to be involved in some way or another but it would be fruitless to ask him because he would only tell her a lie. Instead, she glowered at him knowingly. Terry tried to outstare her but she gave him such a fierce look that the smirk soon disappeared from his face, and then his lips began to quiver as fear overcame him. Miss Throwpee left it at that and began the lesson.

"Right children," she said. "Today we are going to talk about space, the universe, and anything connected with it. Now, to begin with, does anybody know what a galaxy is?"

Terry Bull was the first to raise his hand, much to Miss Throwpee's surprise.

"Yes, Terry... what is a galaxy?" she asked.

"It's a chocolate bar Miss!" he smugly announced.

There followed a murmur of laughter from his classmates, for they too had all heard of the chocolate bar with the brand name of 'Galaxy'.

Miss Throwpee did not find this particularly amusing but she managed to remain calm.

"Very funny Terry," she said patronisingly. "And I suppose the next thing you would like to mention would be Mars, which is also the brand name of a chocolate bar as well as being a planet? However, if I wanted to talk about a chocolate cosmos I would now be discussing PLANTS with you instead of PLANETS!"

She emphasised these words because she was beginning to lose her cool, but everyone in the classroom stared at Miss Throwpee blankly because they did not have a clue what she was talking about. Miss Throwpee realised this, of course, and she went on to explain.

"A chocolate cosmos, children, is the name of a plant belonging to the dahlia family that has brown flowers, and a cosmos is another name for the universe as a whole. So, being as the subject of chocolate had been mentioned, I thought that I would make a joke about it – a play on words really – but, as nobody is laughing, I guess that it is not very funny, or perhaps you are all simply too young to understand... Perhaps we could be a little more serious about this subject from now on though. Therefore, I shall ask the question again: does anybody know what a galaxy is?"

This time, Amanda put her hand in the air first.

"It's a large cluster of stars that can't be seen clearly with the naked eye, Miss," she said.

"Very good Amanda, I am very impressed," said Miss Throwpee. "Now, can anyone name a well-known galaxy for me?"

Amanda raised her hand for a second time.

"The only well-known galaxy that I know of is the Milky Way," she proudly stated.

"That's the name of a chocolate bar too," Terry Bull interrupted, and then he burst into spasms of cackling laughter.

This was the last straw as far as Miss Throwpee was concerned because, since the beginning of term, Terry Bull had constantly disturbed her lessons and now she was at the end of her tether.

"We'll come back to this subject in just a moment Amanda," the teacher said, in an unusually sweet voice for her, as she slowly raised herself up from her chair.

When Miss Throwpee stood up she wore a tight-lipped expression, which was a warning sign that she was about to explode, and her face was beginning to turn purple with rage. Then she stormed across the room and banged her hands down hard on Terry's desk before slowly lowering her head until her purple face was just inches away from his. In stark contrast, the colour had completely drained from Terry's face.

"I have had just about all the insubordination I can take from you young man. If I hear another peep out of you during this lesson I will take you straight to the head teacher's office... IS THAT UNDERSTOOD?" she bellowed.

Although he was a troublemaker Terry was far from stupid and he knew when he had been beaten. A look of sheer terror had suddenly filled the boy's expression whilst his entire body quaked with fear.

Very sheepishly, he nodded his head to acknowledge that he fully understood Miss Throwpee's threat and she then returned to her desk.

In the meantime, Skelly had been beneath Amanda's desk recovering from his ordeal, nursing his wounds which he had received during his battering. He was thoroughly annoyed at being kicked around the room and he was even more annoyed that Amanda had become so upset by the school bullies. But now he was livid because Terry Bull had insulted his home galaxy by comparing it with a chocolate bar. This had suddenly become personal as far as he was concerned and Skelly sought revenge, so he had immediately started to hatch a plan.

He was positioned on the floor directly behind Terry's chair and he realised that, if he could shift the weight of the books that he was carrying in his backpack body, it would be possible to fall forwards and bite the boy's ankles. It took Skelly three attempts to shift the weight of the books but he eventually felt them topple, one at a time, against his back. With that task done he then fell forwards to where Terry's feet were tucked beneath his chair and, at that same moment, Skelly opened his mouth wide and sunk his teeth into Terry's right ankle.

"Now, where was I before I was rudely interrupted?" asked Miss Throwpee in her usual stern voice, once she had settled back down at her desk again. "Oh, yes – the Milky Way... For the second time you are quite correct Amanda. Now, do you know anything about the Milky Way?"

Before Amanda could answer there was a high-pitched scream as Terry Bull leapt from his chair and began to enact a strange dance around the floor on one foot, whereupon the entire class gawped at Terry in utmost bewilderment, wondering what kind of stunt he was trying to pull this time.

"What on Earth is the matter with you child?" Miss Throwpee demanded to know.

Terry pointed to Amanda's backpack that was now laying face-down on the floor.

"*IT BIT ME... THE BAG BIT ME!*" he ranted.

Every one of his classmates instantly erupted into hysterical laughter. But Miss Throwpee could not take any more and she blew her top.

"Right, that does it!" she thundered. "I've never heard anything so ridiculous in all of my life... BAGS DON'T BITE... Go to the principal's office this minute."

"But it did – It really did bite me Miss," Terry protested.

Not wanting to hear any more of his nonsense, Miss Throwpee grabbed Terry by his ear and dragged him from the room.

"Ow... Ouch... Oooh!" was all the children could hear as Terry was forcibly led along the corridor... and how the children all howled with laughter at this.

"Good old Skelly," muttered Amanda as she picked up her backpack and gave him a big hug. "There is some justice after all."

When Miss Throwpee returned to the classroom the topic of conversation about the Milky Way was resumed and the form teacher found herself quite astonished by Amanda's knowledge of the subject. As a reward for her brilliant effort Amanda gained three gold stars and she went home later that day an extremely happy young girl. When she walked past the principal's office as she left school Amanda saw Terry Bull toiling away with a pen in his hand and several sheets of paper in front of him, while Miss de Meana – the head teacher – hovered menacingly over him. Amanda found out at a later date that Terry had been forced to stay behind for detention and write the words *'I must not say stupid things'* one thousand times, and she believed that he thoroughly deserved his punishment and maybe he would think twice about bullying anyone in the future.

Poor Skelly was tired out from his day's outing to school and he could hardly keep his eyes open when they arrived home. Amanda placed the backpack on top of her wardrobe – which Skelly found to be the most comfortable spot in the bedroom – and he promptly fell asleep. Before he drifted off he had told Amanda that he now realised school was for human children and not for little aliens like him, therefore it would be a long time before he went to school with her again. Amanda agreed with him and promised that wherever she took him she would never let such a terrible thing happen to him ever again.

CHAPTER SEVEN

The Lucky Mascot

When Amanda arrived home from school on the following evening she thought that she would treat Skelly to a bath because he was still covered in grime from his previous day's ordeal, but when she burst into her bedroom there was no sign of him. She searched for him in his favourite spot on top of the wardrobe, under her bed and amongst her cuddly toys, but all to no avail because, after hunting high and low, it became obvious that he was nowhere to be found. This was most odd and it puzzled Amanda greatly, so she went downstairs to seek her mother who was in the kitchen preparing the evening meal.

"Mum, have you seen my backpack?" asked Amanda.

"Oh, hello Amanda, how are you? I'm fine, thank you for asking... And, yes, I've had a good day too, how about you?"

Amanda ignored her mum's sarcasm and asked her again if she had seen her backpack.

"If you mean that mangy old rabbit thing... yes, I have seen it," Mum replied.

Amanda's eyes lit up.

"Oh, good," she said, feeling quite relieved. "Where is it?"

"I took it to the rubbish dump today."

Amanda was horrified.

"What?!! You did what? "Why did you take it to the dump?"

"I decided to tidy your bedroom while you were at school – it was in such a state – and, while I was in there, I threw away some of your old stuff that was well-past its sell-by date."

"But my backpack is new; it wasn't old at all," Amanda protested.

"Well, that tatty old thing certainly looked old to me. It was grubby, as well as being frayed at the edges, and there is no point in keeping rubbish."

"It just needed a wash," Amanda argued. "I was going to clean it tonight but now I can't. How do we get it back from the dump?"

"Oh, don't be so ridiculous!" Mum snorted. "I expect it has gone into the incinerator by now, or it has surely been buried under tons of rubbish."

As soon as she heard this, Amanda became grief-stricken and she burst into tears. How could such a thing have happened, she wondered, especially after she had promised Skelly that she would never let anything terrible happen to him ever again?

"But we must get it back, we really must... Please Mum, take me to the rubbish dump," Amanda implored.

"No! Don't you understand me when I say 'No'? It's too late Amanda, your backpack has gone. If you think that I'm going to be sifting through grotty old rubbish, then you've got another thing coming."

Amanda sobbed even harder upon hearing this. Sometimes her mother could be quite mercenary, she thought, although it was not really her fault that she was so house-proud. If anything, Amanda should have given it more thought and advised Skelly to hide during the day when she was not around. Anyway, there was nothing the girl could do to change things, so she decided to retreat to her bedroom because she knew that it was going to be futile to argue with her mum, for this would not resolve matters.

As it turned out, her father had returned home from work early that day and he had heard the tail-end of the conversation between the pair of them. He then followed Amanda into her bedroom because he had realised that there was something special about her backpack and that it meant a lot to her.

"Come on," he said softly, "get your shoes on. I'll take you to the rubbish dump and we'll see if we can find your precious backpack."

Amanda immediately cheered up.

"Oh, thank you Daddy," she said enthusiastically, "but we must hurry, there's no time to waste."

But, after spending quite some time rummaging around the rubbish dump, there was no sign of the missing backpack. Her father had remarked that it was like trying to find a needle in a haystack and decided to call it a day; therefore, he and Amanda returned home empty-handed.

Amanda was very restless that night, tossing and turning all the while as she worried about Skelly's whereabouts, wondering whether she would ever see him again. She was indeed a very unhappy child now that her little friend was missing, and this made her feel terrible because she blamed herself for his loss.

She had also lost her appetite and, on the morning following Skelly's disappearance, she moped over her breakfast cereal, dragging her spoon lazily around the bowl as she stared into its soggy depths. Without eating so much as a tiny morsel, Amanda pushed the bowl aside and quietly put on her coat as she got ready to go to school. Then, at the very moment she stepped out of the front door, a garbage truck arrived to take away the weekly rubbish.

"Mornin' Amanda," said Mr Grubb and Mr Black in unison.

"Hullo," she grunted at the two dustmen in a mournful voice.

In a complete hazy daydream, Amanda walked past the two jovial dustmen without so much as looking up, but then something made her stop dead in her tracks. She had heard a faint noise which sounded like a voice quietly calling out her name.

"A-m-an-daa," it said in a slow, drawn-out sort of way.

The perplexed schoolgirl spun this way and that, looking all around to try and find out who was calling her, but there was nobody to be seen except for the two dustmen who now had their backs to her, so it could not possibly have been them who were calling her name. Having pricked up her ears Amanda listened hard, believing that she was going mad, but, sure enough, she heard the voice again.

"A-m-an-daa," repeated the mysterious voice.

There was definitely nobody else in sight of where she was standing, so she walked around to the front of the truck where she distinctly heard the voice for a third time.

"A-M-AN-DA!" came the pathetic little sound as it strained harder to make itself heard.

It was only then that she noticed the tatty-looking mascot that was tied to the front of the truck with bale twine. It was quite usual for dustmen to pin a mascot to the front of their vehicle – often an old teddy bear or another cuddly toy that someone no longer had any use for – and there was something familiar about this particular one, but she could not put her finger on exactly what it was. All of a sudden, the mascot raised its head and rolled its eyes around and, although this made her jump, Amanda realised that it was none other than Skelly! She had not recognised him until now because he had become even dirtier-looking than ever and he was losing his white colouring through lack of milk.

"Oh, you poor thing!" Amanda exclaimed. "What have they done to you? Wait just a minute and I'll free you."

However, it was not quite as simple as that, because Amanda was aware that Skelly was now the property of the dustmen and it was not the done thing to take him without asking. So, she approached one of the men.

"Please could I have the bunny rabbit that's tied to the front of your lorry Mr Grubb?" Amanda asked.

"Well lass, I don't really know about that," said Mr Grubb. "We found it on the rubbish dump only yesterday evening and we thought that it would make an ideal lucky mascot for our truck."

Amanda gave a deep sigh and lowered her head despondently, whereupon Mr Grubb could see that the young girl was a little upset.

"Why do you want it?" he asked.

"Because he used to be mine but my mum threw him away yesterday by mistake when she was tidying my bedroom," Amanda explained.

"Seems a shame to have to part with it," said Mr Grubb. "We quite like the look of him, you know. There's something a bit different about a little floppy rabbit – it's not the sort of thing you come across every day. Mind you, it has become dirty really fast; it was a dull grey colour yesterday evening but it has become almost transparent today and you can nearly see his bones... What do you think Mr Black, shall we hand it over?"

"Aw, go on. Let the young lady 'ave her bunny rabbit back," said Mr Black. "We can always find another one to go on the front of the truck. Besides, you know they don't last for very long anyway, being exposed to the elements and all that road dirt."

Mr Grubb immediately untied the rabbit backpack and handed

him to Amanda. She was so delighted that she made both of the men's day by giving them a big peck on their cheeks before rushing into the house to give Skelly some revitalising milk. Within moments the tiny alien's skin returned to a much healthier shade of near white, although he was still in desperate need of a bath.

"You are indeed a lucky little mascot Skelly," Amanda told him. "It is really nice to have you home again; I've missed you so much."

She hugged Skelly tightly, and then she kissed him lovingly before placing him in his favourite spot on top of the wardrobe so that he could get some well-needed rest. When this was done, she rushed downstairs to tell her parents the glad tidings.

Mum did not seem at all interested in her daughter's joyous news. Actually, she was far more concerned with the fact that Amanda had now missed the school bus. However, her father was a little more sympathetic.

"It's not the end of the world, love," he said to his wife. "Don't fret over it; I'll drop Amanda off at the school on my way past because I don't have to be at work until later this morning.

Mum seemed quite relieved at this suggestion and she turned her attention to Amanda.

"I apologise for being such a grouch at the moment sweetheart. I think it's because of the stress and strain I've been under during the house move. I really am pleased that you've found your backpack again," said Mum, lifting up Amanda and giving her a big hug.

"That's okay Mum, I still love you all the same," Amanda said with a smile, at the same time returning a hug and a kiss. "All's well that ends well, eh?"

CHAPTER EIGHT

An Embarrassing Mistake

It was the first day of the summer holidays and Amanda felt excited for two reasons. Firstly, there was no school for six weeks, which meant that she could get out of bed when she pleased; and, secondly, she was going on a trip to the coast that very afternoon.

Amanda rushed downstairs and into the kitchen to be greeted by the odour of freshly-ground coffee. She hated that smell. It was on her list of the top ten most dreadful smells in the world as far as she was concerned and she could not understand why adults enjoyed it so much, believing that it must taste exactly the same as it smelled – yucky!

"Have you seen my bucket and spade?" asked Amanda in a rather nasally voice, as she pinched her nose with her finger and thumb in an attempt to drown out the smell.

Mum was pouring coffee into two mugs. She placed the coffee pot back onto the work surface and put her hands on her hips in a despairing manner. But, before she could open her mouth to say anything, Amanda let out a huge sigh, thrust her arms down by her side and began to giggle. Then she hurriedly ran over to her mother, throwing her arms around her in a warm embrace.

"Sorry Mum," she apologised. "Good morning... How are you

this morning? Did you sleep well?" Then she gave a low curtsy and began to giggle again.

Dad watched this scene with amusement and began to chuckle also. Then Mum saw the funny side of things and she joined in too, bending down to squeeze Amanda tightly as she hugged her.

"No I haven't seen your bucket and spade sweetheart, but I expect it's somewhere in the garage where it has been since our last summer holiday."

"Thanks," said Amanda, quickly breaking free of her mother's bear-hug and making a dash towards the back door.

"You can go and find your blessed bucket and spade in a while," Mum told her. "Eat your breakfast first."

Amanda pouted her lips in disappointment as she turned to face her mother.

"Oh, let her get them now," Dad intervened. "It won't hurt for her to have breakfast afterwards; we've got all morning before we leave for the coast anyway."

"Okay, very well then," Mum surrendered. "But don't be too long because I've got to pack the suitcases yet and I don't want to spend the whole morning in the kitchen slaving over breakfast."

Amanda's brief look of disappointment faded away and she darted outside, grinning from ear to ear. She returned five minutes later with her bucket and spade in her hands.

"The milkman is late today, isn't he?" Amanda casually mentioned when she came back into the kitchen.

"I don't know, I haven't been to fetch the milk in yet," Mum replied. "Why do you ask?"

"When I went out to the garage I could see his milk float parked on the driveway," she replied.

Mum glanced at the clock that hung on the kitchen wall. It was a quarter after eight and the milkman had usually been and gone by seven o'clock.

"Yes, he is late today," she said. "I expect there is a good reason for it though."

"There's a reason for everything," Dad commented without looking up from his morning paper.

Amanda and her mother exchanged puzzled looks, wondering what on Earth he had meant by his philosophical meanderings.

"Mind your own business!" Mum said out of the blue.

This remark made Dad glance up from his magazine with a surprised expression on his face, but the cheeky grin on his wife's face told him that she was pulling his leg. Amanda had tensed momentarily because she also thought that her mother was being serious, but, when she realised that she was joking, she relaxed and sat down at the kitchen table to eat her cereal, feeling quite pleased that Mum was acting more like her usual self.

"Would you like some more coffee Bill?" asked his wife as she offered him the coffee pot.

"Not just now, thanks love. I'll get some when I'm ready."

"What about you Amanda? Would you like some coffee?"

Amanda looked at her mother in disgust. She knew that Amanda hated the smell of coffee and had never dared to taste it for that very reason.

"Mmm, lovely coffee... What a beautiful aroma," said Mum, deliberately teasing Amanda as she wafted the steam from the coffee pot around with her hands to send it drifting in her daughter's direction.

"Ha-ha!" retorted Amanda, rather sarcastically, although she thought how nice it was to see her mother in such a jovial mood.

Dad suddenly stirred from his chair and decided to pour himself a mug of coffee after all.

"I'd better have another refill now, before one of you knocks it over; and then nobody will be able to have any," he complained.

After he had poured out his coffee he stood by the kitchen window whilst sipping his hot drink, peering down the long driveway, apparently deep in thought.

"The milkman seems to be taking a long time to deliver the milk. Does it usually take him ten minutes to place a couple of bottles on the ground?" he enquired.

"Is he still there?" his wife asked, her voice taking on an anxious tone.

"Maybe his milk float has broken down," Dad suggested. "I'll take a wander to the end of the drive and see what's happening."

Mum's face had turned white.

"No, it's alright – I'll go," she hurriedly said, the last words of her sentence barely audible as she slammed the door behind her.

Amanda and her father exchanged bewildered glances as they watched her bound along the driveway, like a gazelle being chased by a lion, until she reached the stationary milk float where she stopped to take a rest. Here, as Mum surveyed the scene, it was obvious there was no sign of the milkman, but then the full reality of the situation began to sink in and she put her hands over her face in disbelief. You see, although she had been told that the Milk Bandit had been around for years and nobody was really bothered too much about it, she could not come to terms with the fact that bottles of milk kept disappearing and nothing was ever done to prevent it; therefore, she had set another one of her traps!

During the previous evening she had dug a large hole in the ground (around six feet deep by six feet square) in an area next to where the milkman always deposited the milk when he delivered it. She marked an 'X' on the ground with chalk where she had assumed would be the best place to dig, but then she changed her mind because she realised this spot would be too obvious to the thief. So, she then marked another 'X' and dug the hole at this point instead. When the task was complete, she covered the hole with a thin sheet of plywood and placed a layer of soil over the top of it, mixed together with leaves and twigs so that it blended in with the surroundings. Before disguising the hole, she thoughtfully dropped in a pile of cushions so that the thief would not injure themselves when they fell. And then she threw in two packets of chocolate cookies and a bottle of water so that the captive would not be hungry or thirsty.

When Dave the milkman had arrived to deliver the milk that morning, he bent down to place the bottles in their usual spot, but he suspected that something was not quite right after noticing that a large 'X' had been drawn on the ground nearby. Realising that someone had obviously tried to erase it, he sensed that a trap had been set and he quickly stepped aside. Suddenly, to Dave's horror, the ground unexpectedly caved in and the next thing he knew was that he was lying in a deep hole on a bed of cushions and broken cookies. He also found himself covered from head to toe in soil, leaves and twigs. Slightly dazed, Dave dusted himself down and stood up but, not being very tall and a little overweight also, he could not pull himself out of the hole and so he had to remain there until help came his way.

And there he stayed until now, when Amanda's mother peered into the hole rather nervously and saw Dave's ruddy face staring back at her. She thought he seemed quite comfortable sitting there, cross-legged on his bed of cushions whilst chomping away on a broken cookie, but Mum was aware that, if nothing else, at least his pride must have been hurt. When he saw her, Dave tilted the peak of his cap politely, although he remained silent for there was nothing that needed to be said.

"I... I'll give m-m-my husband a c-c-call and get h-h-him to help you out of t-t-there," Mum stammered as she grimaced shamefully.

But, after walking away from the edge of the hole, she returned only a few seconds later and she was acting rather awkwardly.

"Er... I've left my mobile... um... 'phone in the house," she said. "You don't happen to have one I can borrow do you?"

Dave pointed over the top of the hole.

"There's one in me milk float," he said calmly.

With that, she went to fetch Dave's mobile 'phone from his vehicle and then immediately called her husband.

"Bill!" she said in an urgent voice. "Would you please bring a set of stepladders to the end of the driveway – I'll explain later. And... please hurry!"

Then she turned to Dave and nonchalantly commented that he had several missed calls on his mobile 'phone and she would hand it to him.

"S'probably the dairy wondering where Oi've got to," said Dave, as he reached up to take the 'phone from her.

But, as Mum stretched out her arm towards him, she trod on one of the milk bottles that Dave had dropped before he fell into the hole. Then, as the bottle rolled beneath her foot, she lost her balance, which caused her to fall head-first into the hole and land on top of him. With their faces just inches apart they remained thus – pinned in together like sardines in a tin – for the next few moments while they tried to separate themselves in the confined space. Eventually, after much struggling, the luckless pair managed to untangle themselves.

"I'm sure help will be here in a short while," Mum said rather hopefully.

"Oi've waited this long, another few minutes ain't gonna be neither here nor there missus," Dave replied in a slightly agitated voice.

Sure enough, no sooner had she said this when Dad arrived on the scene with Amanda in tow. When they had got over their initial surprise at finding the pair of them in such close proximity in a hole in the ground, there was much sniggering as they fought hard to hold the ladder steady whilst the two 'captives' climbed out. Once she was free, Mum hung her head in shame and tried to shield her eyes from everyone's gaze in order to hide her embarrassment, while Dave did not seem in the least bit bothered by his experience. Remarkably, his pure white smile had already returned to his face.

"I was only trying to catch the Milk Bandit," Mum tried to explain.

"It was a fair attempt, Oi'll give yer that," Dave said with a chuckle.

"I'm really sorry," she said.

"No real arm done missus... Oi'd better be off now 'cause I'm a little behind schedule. G'day to y'all."

Dave tilted the peak of his cap politely and set off in the direction of his milk float, and when he walked past Amanda the jovial milkman turned towards her.

"She'll never catch 'im y'know," he whispered, and then he winked at her knowingly before returning to his milk float to drive away as fast as the little battery-powered cart could possibly go.

The subject of Mum's latest escapade was not mentioned by anyone for the remainder of that day but, during the long car journey to the coast, Amanda would occasionally have an attack of the giggles which was followed by a lengthy spell of chuckling from her father, and both of them would then shake uncontrollably. Mum was quite aware that they were quietly laughing at her failed bid to capture the Milk Bandit, but she dared not say a word for she knew she would never hear the last of it.

CHAPTER NINE

Lost Property

It seemed to take forever and a day to drive down to the coast, during which time Amanda quickly became bored. Together with her father, she had played 'I-Spy', 'The Admiral's Cat' and just about every other game that she could think of, but then she had run out of things to do. Meanwhile, Mum had been concentrating on driving; therefore, she could only join in occasionally.

"Are we nearly there yet?" Amanda asked for the umpteenth time.

"Yes, we're nearly there. Only another ten minutes to go," Mum told her.

"But you've been saying that for ages and we still keep travelling," moaned Amanda.

"Oh, for goodness sake, give it a rest Amanda! We left home four hours ago and since then we have had to stop when you needed to use the loo, and then again because you were hungry, and for a third time because you felt travel sick... Is it any wonder that we are still on the way there?"

"I wasn't actually sick though..." Amanda began, but she was quickly interrupted by her father.

"Chill out girls, we're going on holiday. Can't you call a truce between the pair of you, just for once, and enjoy the moment?" asked Dad in a calm voice.

Neither of his female travelling companions gave an answer but there followed a peaceful silence for the next few miles. However, this was short-lived because Amanda suddenly burst into tears.

"Oh, no! I've forgotten my backpack," she wailed. "I put it down when we stopped to eat at the motorway service station. We'll have to go back and get it."

"Don't be so ridiculous," Mum snapped at her. "The service station we stopped at is miles away now and someone will surely have taken your bag by this time. You'll have to buy another one with your holiday spending money instead."

"I don't want to buy another backpack – I *have* to get that one back," Amanda stipulated.

But Mum was adamant.

"Well, you can't. We've driven too far now, we're not going back and that's final," she said.

Dad came to the rescue once again.

"Whoa, whoa, whoa – hold your horses," he said, directing his sentence at both of them. "Let us at least discuss this matter in a civilized manner without arguing."

Then he turned to speak to his wife.

"We are only ten minutes from our holiday cottage right now – I'll drop you off and take Amanda back to the services myself. It's only about an hour's journey each way so we'll be gone for a couple of hours, that's all."

"If you don't mind taking Amanda back to the restaurant, that will be great," said Mum. "I'm exhausted and I need to rest. I don't think I can stay awake much longer."

So, with this decision finalised, Mum was left at the holiday cottage to get some rest, while Amanda and her father set off in the direction of the service station in the hope that her backpack would be found.

Meanwhile, poor Skelly was feeling quite rejected because he had been overlooked. Amanda had taken off her backpack at the service station and placed it on the floor beside her table, just as she had said, but she and her parents had left in a bit of a rush and had completely forgotten to pick him up. Helpless to do anything about the situation, Skelly had watched the whole family depart.

"Hey! What about me?" he said to himself, although he was sure that Amanda would return at any moment to retrieve him. But he waited and waited, and Amanda still did not come back.

He had only been alone for a short while when a boy's voice that came from right behind him suddenly made Skelly aware that he had been spotted and, in that same instance, he found himself hoisted into the air.

"Look what I've found," said the triumphant boy.

"I saw it first. I've had my eye on it for ages. Give it to me!" demanded the boy's brother, and he tried to snatch the backpack away from him.

Skelly was tugged first one way and then the other as the two brothers argued over their find – it was a good thing that his limbs could stretch, otherwise they would have been pulled clean out of their sockets. Luckily for him, he was rescued by the boys' mother, who stepped in just at the right moment when Skelly was as full stretching point. She immediately pulled the backpack away from the two boys and gave each of them a clip around the ears with one swipe of her other hand.

"It doesn't belong to either of you," she said. "Some poor child has forgotten to pick up this lovely backpack and I'm sure their heart will be broken. Therefore, we shall have to do the decent thing and hand it in to the Lost Property Department."

The scowling brothers rubbed their sore ears as their mother marched them away with her.

"Hmm, serves them right. Those boys certainly deserved their punishment," thought Skelly as his aching limbs finally settled back to their normal length, to remould into the shoulder straps of the backpack.

When they arrived at the Lost Property desk the attitude of the female clerk was very frosty towards them as the backpack was handed over.

"If nobody has claimed it in a year's time, then it's yours," said the sour-faced old prune, knowing full well that they would have forgotten all about the bag by that time. "Sign here, and leave your address too."

The miserable clerk thus handed over a crumpled-up piece of paper, whereupon Skelly's finder left her details and departed with her two disappointed sons.

As soon as they had walked away, the clerk opened a large cupboard door that was located behind her and she threw the backpack inside without even looking. Skelly hit the wall with considerable force before dropping onto a coat-hook that he had been purposely flung upon by the woman, and the door was then slammed shut behind him. As he helplessly hung there – by his straps in the dark interior of the cupboard – he pondered what to do next, wondering how he was going to get out of this scrape. However, a short while later, the cupboard door re-opened and the voluminous figure of the sour-faced old prune filled its frame. She stared at the backpack for a few moments, whilst deep in thought, and then muttered something out loud.

"Why the heck should I let those people have this backpack? It's quite a nice one, so I think I'll take it home with me. After all, finders-keepers."

With that, she tore up the piece of paper that contained the real finder's name and address and then she reached forward to roughly remove Skelly from the wall, pulling the coat-hook from its fixing point at the same time. What was he going to do now, he wondered, for he was in an even worse predicament than before and he did not know which was the lesser of the two evils: being taken home by this mean woman or being handed over to the two rowdy boys?"

Well, as luck would have it, when the sour-faced old prune left her workplace and walked through the car park she happened to pass Amanda and her father who had just arrived at the service station to see if her backpack was still there.

"Hey, there's Skelly!" exclaimed Amanda, when she caught sight of the woman who was dragging the backpack along the ground behind her.

"Who on Earth is Skelly?" asked her father.

"Oh, that's the name that I've given to my backpack," Amanda quickly replied. "Hurry Dad, we must go after that woman before she gets into her car and drives away with him."

After giving chase across the tarmac, they managed to catch up with the clerk and confront her just as she reached her car.

"Excuse me madam, but I think that's my daughter's backpack you've got there," Dad politely said.

The woman looked him up and down distastefully as if he was a piece of trash.

"No, it isn't," she sneered.

"Yes, it is," Amanda corrected her. "I left it here by mistake earlier this afternoon and I know that the backpack is mine because I would recognise it anywhere."

"I think you must be mistaken... I've had this bag for a few weeks now," lied the Lost Property clerk, "so get out of my way, I want to go home."

At that moment, the manageress of the service station appeared on the scene. She had just finished working her shift and was approaching her own car when she heard the commotion that the argumentative clerk was causing.

"Sorry to interrupt," she said, addressing herself to Amanda's dad, "but I am the manageress of these premises – maybe I can be of some assistance to you. What seems to be the problem here?"

"I've just been accused by this hoodlum of stealing his brat's – I mean, his daughter's – backpack," the no-good clerk ranted.

"Well, you are stealing it... and it is my backpack," Amanda insisted.

"Prove it!" said the clerk, spitting all over the place as she talked.

"I can prove it too," Amanda said enthusiastically. "If you open up the bag you will find a pencil case with my name – Amanda James – written on it; and a summer hat also, with a name badge sewn inside."

The horrified clerk's eyes grew larger as the possible repercussions of this statement sunk in, and she hurriedly tried to worm her way out of the situation.

"Well, it is possible that I have picked up the wrong bag by mistake..." she began to say, but before she could finish her sentence the manageress asked Amanda if she would mind if she looked inside the backpack in order to settle the matter once and for all.

The clerk reluctantly handed over the backpack and, sure enough, the manageress found a pencil case inside with Amanda's name on it, together with a summer hat, just as she had said. The manageress looked at her employee in disgust.

"The only thing I have to say to you, Miss Warr-Monga, is that your behaviour has been despicable and I will not accept such dishonesty within the company. It therefore leaves me with no option other than to dismiss you from this employment on the spot. In other words – *YOU'RE FIRED!*"

"Take your rotten bag and stick your rotten job," sneered the dishonest clerk.

Then she threw herself into her car and sped away, never to be seen again. After the clerk had gone, the manageress turned towards Amanda and her father to apologise profusely.

"I am truly sorry about the deplorable behaviour of one of my former staff members and I shall make sure that nothing like this ever happens again. On behalf of this service station: please bring your family for a slap-up meal in our restaurant whenever you wish, as a token of our humble apologies."

With that, the manageress generously produced a thick wad of meal vouchers. Having accepted the offer, Amanda and her father returned to their car and set off on their return journey to the holiday cottage where they found Mum waiting on the doorstep to greet them upon their arrival.

"We've found Skelly!" Dad excitedly exclaimed as soon as he got out of the car.

"Who, in the name of thunder, is Skelly?" asked Mum.

"Oh, that's the name of Amanda's backpack – that's what she has called her rabbit," Dad replied, patting Skelly firmly on the head. "It's great to have him back."

"How do you know that it is a he?"

"He has to be, because only boys get up to such mischief," Dad answered.

"I've heard it all now," Mum said with a grin on her face. "You'll be saying that he has a mind of his own next!"

"Oh, but I think he probably has," Dad chuckled.

Amanda had been absorbed with other things while this conversation was going on, although she was listening just the same. She felt extremely pleased to be reunited with Skelly and, as she hugged him close to her heart, she wondered whether her father suspected that something was not quite normal about her backpack, or if he was only saying this in a light-hearted manner. Whatever the reason, she imagined that she would probably find out one day soon.

CHAPTER TEN

The Pirates of Penn Sands

The holiday cottage was situated in a lovely position overlooking the picturesque bay of Penn Sands, with its craggy cliffs which towered high above the soft white sand that made up its beach.

After a dull and drizzly start to the first morning of Amanda's summer holiday, the skies eventually cleared to pave the way for glorious sunshine, together with rising temperatures. Once the weather had improved, she and her parents made their way down the winding path that led to the beach. It was lunchtime when they arrived on the beach, by which time it was already packed with holidaymakers; however, they did manage to find a suitable spot where they could sit down and have a picnic. Amanda loved picnics and she could hardly wait to tuck into this one because she had packed her favourite sandwiches, namely freshly-sliced banana with cheese and onion flavour crisps – Yummy! Then, after her meal had gone down, she decided to build a sandcastle.

It turned out that the sand was too dry and powdery for this task so Amanda chose to go for a paddle in the sea instead, taking her backpack with her so that Skelly did not get mislaid. When she got to the water's edge there were lots of children splashing about in the sea, some of whom were floating lazily around on comfortable-looking airbeds.

"I wish that I had an airbed, it looks like so much fun," Amanda whispered longingly to Skelly.

Having already observed these children playing happily on their airbeds, Skelly quickly offered to make Amanda's wish come true.

"If you can find somewhere out of sight where I can change shape, then I am positive that I can become an airbed too and you can have just as much fun as they are having," he said.

With this in mind, Amanda immediately began to look for somewhere private and, when she had located a secluded spot, she disappeared behind a cluster of large rocks with Skelly. When she stepped back onto the beach again she carried with her a fancy white airbed with rabbit facial features, and she told her parents that she was going to play in the sea on it.

"Take care that the tide doesn't turn," Dad warned her, "or else you could be carried out to sea."

Amanda waved in reply, as if she had heard what her father had said, but she was already heading towards the shoreline and was not really listening. Her mother had been lying down on a reclining sun-bed while they were having this conversation and she glanced up momentarily, tilting her sunglasses back onto her head.

"Where did Amanda get that airbed?" she asked.

"I don't know. I assume that she must have brought it with her," replied Dad.

"I don't remember seeing it when I packed her suitcase," Mum commented as she placed her sunglasses over her eyes again and then lay back down.

Having kept a beady eye on Amanda in the sweltering heat for quite some time to ensure that she remained safe, her father had a sudden hankering for an ice-cream.

"I'm going to fetch some ice-creams from the parlour at the end of the promenade," he announced. "Will you keep an eye on Amanda while I'm gone?"

"Yes, of course I will; she'll be fine with me," Mum sleepily replied.

And, with that, Dad set off in search of ice-creams. Meanwhile, Amanda was having a thoroughly enjoyable time on her new airbed, and so too was Skelly. He was experiencing the time of his life because, in all the years he had been stranded on Earth, he had never been in the sea before.

"*Shiddleydootz!* This is great fun," he enthused.

"Yes, isn't it just," agreed Amanda as they splashed about in the water.

But, after a while, they both became very tired due to a combination of excitement, together with the heat of the afternoon sun, and the splashing about began to cease when Amanda began to drop off to sleep. For some time she lay upon the airbed with her fingers and toes dangling in the warm surface water as they bobbed up and down on the gentle swell. There were no other children playing nearby so Skelly chose this quiet moment to talk to Amanda.

"I'm a bit concerned about your father," he said. "Do you think he knows that I'm not really a backpack?"

"No... I reckon that he's quite interested in you but he doesn't suspect anything," she reassured him.

"Then how do you explain the fact that when he thinks no-one is looking he touches me and pinches my flesh?" asked Skelly. "It's quite undignified you know."

"Maybe he just likes the feel of your skin. After all, he believes you are made from some kind of material that he has never come across before. Don't you remember the first time he set eyes upon you in my bedroom Skelly, when he said how strange your skin felt to his touch?"

"Only too well," Skelly replied. "He almost broke my neck! Anyway, that's beside the point... I still find the touching thing a little disconcerting all the same. Is there no privacy any more?"

Amanda laughed at this remark.

"Stop worrying about it Skelly. I really don't think there is anything in it," she said.

A few moments later, Amanda's struggling voice faded away when she fell asleep. The sound of her gentle snoring made Skelly feel tired too and, very soon, he also drifted off to sleep. But, while they dozed, the tide changed direction and they slowly began to ebb out to sea.

When Amanda's father returned with two delicious-looking ice-creams – each one containing a large piece of chocolate and covered in strawberry syrup, with tiny pieces of coloured candy sprinkled over the top – he found that his wife was sound asleep. He scanned the beach but there was no sign of Amanda or her airbed, so he shook her mother roughly in order to wake her up.

"How long have you been asleep?" he asked in an agitated voice. "There is no sign of Amanda anywhere."

His wife instantly sprang from her sun-bed and she too surveyed the shoreline as far as the horizon to confirm the fact that Amanda was definitely nowhere to be seen.

"I... I must have dozed off," she said in a shaky voice. "I can't have been asleep for more than a few minutes though, so she can't be far away. Perhaps she's found someone on the beach to play with."

"She knows that we have always warned her to stay away from strangers. But, at the end of the day, she is only a kid and if she has found a new friend of her own age then you may well be right," Dad said with his voice filled with hope.

After he had made this statement their eyes swept around the crowded beach, but there were so many people present it was impossible to see if Amanda was amongst them.

"She could be anywhere," Dad said at length. "There's only one thing for it – we'll have to go our separate ways to search for her… Oh, here's your ice-cream by the way; I've already eaten mine. You had better take Amanda's along with you before I get tempted to eat that as well."

He handed his wife the remainder of a melted lump of ice-cream with two wafer cones sticking out of it, and then he departed in a rush. She stared at the sticky mess in disgust and tossed it on the beach to give the seagulls a feast before setting off in the opposite direction to her husband.

Following a brief nap, Amanda awoke to find that she was adrift. She had no idea where she was at first and, thinking that she was in her own bed at home, she almost fell off the airbed and into the sea. When it finally dawned on her what had happened she started to panic.

"Wake up Skelly," she yelled at the top of her voice.

Skelly stirred and rolled his eyes about him, trying to focus through his blurred vision.

"Oh dear," he said in dismay, "I think we have a problem."

They had drifted almost half-a-mile offshore and the tide was now taking them around the coastline, by which time the crowded beach they had started out from was out of sight because they had rounded the headland.

"What are we going to do now Skelly? I'm scared," Amanda cried.

"Don't be afraid, I'll think of something," Skelly replied, trying to put on a brave face. "Can you swim?"

"No," Amanda flatly told him.

Just at that moment, Skelly spotted a large swell coming towards them that was heading inland, and he had a brainwave.

"Quick Amanda, remove the cap from my air-valve," he ordered.

"What use will that be? As soon as we let the air out you will deflate and then we'll sink," Amanda whimpered.

"Just do it... There's no time to waste."

Somewhat reluctantly, Amanda did exactly as she was told and, at that very same moment, the wave washed beneath them. The escaping air from the airbed then propelled the duo on the crest of the wave until it began to break and the fortunate pair became washed-up on the shore.

"*Shiddleydootz!* That was a lucky break," gasped Skelly.

"More like a lucky breaker," Amanda spluttered. "That was quick thinking Skelly, you have saved our lives. Who knows where we could have ended up?"

"Oh, it was nothing," Skelly replied rather modestly.

Amanda sat on a large rock while she regained her breath, glancing all around her as she tried to figure out where they had ended up.

"I wonder where we are," Amanda muttered, thinking out loud.

"We appear to be in a small, secluded cove," Skelly replied helpfully.

"I can see that," she said, "but there appears to be no way out because the cliffs are too steep to climb. Nobody will ever find us here."

"Hmm, I see your point," agreed Skelly. "Wait a minute... Look over there – isn't that the entrance to a cave?"

She followed Skelly's finger to where he was pointing and, sure enough, there appeared to be a large hole at the base of the cliff where the sea flowed into a small inlet and disappeared from view. Unfortunately, the route across the rocks to get there was going to be very slippery because of the wet seaweed that carpeted them.

"Do you think that you can get across the rocks okay? It's going to be difficult but I know that I can make it," boasted Skelly.

"Of course I can," Amanda said rather indignantly. "Huh! Just because I'm a girl doesn't mean that I can't do anything that boys can. Come on, I'll race you – Let's go!"

Scrambling over the rocks with the agility of a monkey, she led the way and reached the cave ahead of Skelly, to prove her point that girls were just as good as boys at doing things like that – if not better. Here, they hesitated for a moment or two before entering, wondering whether it was such a good idea after all. However, they eventually made up their minds to go in.

It was very dark inside the cave, making it very difficult to see where they were going, but every now and again Amanda noticed some tiny flashes of bright green light that would illuminate for a brief instant and then disappear altogether. She grabbed hold of Skelly and clung onto him tightly.

"Wh-what are those strange glowing lights?" Amanda stammered.

"They are only fireflies," Skelly informed her, "which are

completely harmless little insects whose abdomens light up in an attempt to attract a partner – You know... boyfriend and girlfriend kind of stuff."

She breathed a sigh of relief and let go of Skelly. The pair then continued to tread their way carefully through the cave but, very soon, they came to a dead-end. Amanda was bitterly disappointed.

"This isn't a way out after all," she cried. "We're trapped. What are we going to do now?"

Skelly was a short distance to Amanda's left-hand side at this point, feeling his way along the rocky wall that was now blocking their path, when he suddenly let out a little shriek.

"There's something here," he said. "It feels as if it is made of wood but I can't be sure."

"Maybe it's a gateway or a door," said Amanda in a hopeful voice. "If only we could see inside this dark, musty cave."

"I've just had an idea," said Skelly. "Don't go away."

"Like I'm going to find somewhere to go!" she replied sarcastically. "More to the point... where are you going?"

"Don't worry, I'm not deserting you. I'll be back in a jiffy."

"Skelly? Wh..."

But before Amanda could finish her sentence he had already returned with a handful of fireflies that he had collected, which he then popped into his mouth. Because Skelly's flesh was now turning transparent through lack of milk, every time the fireflies lit up then so did Skelly's face, which illuminated the cave for a few brief seconds at a time and, in the flashing green light, Skelly could see that Amanda's face was a picture of joy.

"What a bright idea Skelly. Bright... get it?" she joked.

How they laughed at that. They roared and roared and each time they laughed the cave glowed because of the fireflies in Skelly's mouth, which made them chuckle even more. In fact, they laughed so much that Skelly suddenly began to hiccup and he accidentally swallowed one of the fireflies, which caused his own abdomen to glow. Of course, this made them laugh harder than ever.

They eventually calmed down enough to take a look around the cave though, and, following a brief inspection, it appeared that the wooden item Skelly had found was actually a wooden crate. And not just one either because, rather mysteriously, it turned out that the entire cave was stacked up to its rocky ceiling with crate upon crate upon crate.

"I wonder what they contain?" said Amanda.

But before they could investigate the matter something forced them to fall silent. It was the sound of an engine, followed by voices that were getting louder as they became nearer.

"Quick, let's hide behind those rocks," Amanda suggested.

Skelly immediately opened his mouth and all of the fireflies flew away, except for the one that was still lodged in his stomach. Amanda had to smack him hard on his back to make him cough up the last firefly, which then flew out of his mouth to leave the cave in complete darkness once again.

Meanwhile, the approaching voices and accompanying footsteps grew louder, and with them came a light that grew brighter all the while until the cave eventually became floodlit. Amanda and Skelly peered out from their hiding places behind the rocks to witness two large, burly men carrying a wooden crate between them, similar to the ones that were already stacked within the cave. They set it down on the ground near to the stockpile and then one of the men raised his lantern and shone it around the cave.

"That's another job well done, Burt," he said in a gruff voice.

"Yeah... Marvellous! We should get a pretty penny for this consignment, eh Charlie?" Burt replied in an equally gruff voice. "No point standing 'ere 'n' starin' at it though. We got a lot to shift yet... C'mon."

The two men turned around and headed back to the cave entrance, swinging their lanterns to and fro and whistling merrily to themselves as they went.

"Who do you think they are?" Skelly whispered to Amanda when they had gone.

"Smugglers or pirates, I guess. I'm not really sure. They must have arrived here by boat though, and that could be our way out of this place. Let's follow them – but be careful so as not to be seen."

Amanda was right, for bobbing up and down gently on the waves just outside the entrance to the cave was a small cabin cruiser. She and Skelly watched as the two smugglers unloaded yet another crate from the boat and then disappeared back into the cave with it.

"There's only one way in and out of here," whispered Amanda, "and that's by sea. Let's take their boat... Hurry up Skelly."

With that, they climbed on board the cabin cruiser, at which point Amanda stared in dismay at the controls because she did not know what to do with them.

"Have you ever driven one of these things before?" she asked.

Skelly shook his head.

"Oh well, here goes," said Amanda as she flicked all of the switches on the instrument panel, one after the other.

The boat's outboard motor had been left running, so as soon as she flicked the switches the engine revved-up, but the cabin cruiser refused to budge.

"What's stopping us from moving?" she screamed, trying to make herself heard over the noisy engine. "We're not going anywhere and we desperately need to get out of here because the smugglers are bound to have heard us by now. What shall we do?"

Right at that very same moment, both of them suddenly spotted a rope that hung from a metal loop on the side of the boat and disappeared into the sea, whereupon they realised that it was an anchor which was preventing the boat from moving. They tugged and pulled at the rope with all of their might and, just as the smugglers came running and shouting from the cave, the anchor freed itself, forcing the boat to shoot forward with a jolt and sending Amanda and Skelly reeling across its deck. Fortunately, Amanda was able to grab the steering wheel, which enabled her to regain her balance and then take control of the cabin cruiser.

"Phew! That was a close call Skelly," Amanda said, but there was no reply.

"*Skelly?*" she repeated in a questioning voice.

Fearing that Skelly had been left behind, she glanced over her shoulder and, to her delight, she saw that he was still there, albeit hanging on to the end of the anchor rope for dear life as he was dragged across the waves in the wake of the boat.

"Hang on tight Skelly!" Amanda yelled encouragingly.

"What do you think I'm doing?" his plaintive reply came back.

In a bit of a quandary as to what to do next, she happened to notice a button on the dashboard that had a symbol showing an anchor, together with an arrow that pointed in an upward direction, so she immediately pressed it to see what would happen. Luckily, it had been the right thing to do because, slowly but surely, the anchor began to retract and with it came Skelly. When he was within her reach Amanda grabbed his hand and she pulled the soggy little alien onto the boat.

"Glad you could make it," Amanda said with a grin on her face.

"Sorry I'm late," Skelly replied. "I thought I would do a spot of water skiing before joining you on board!"

The relieved pair hugged each other fondly and then fell about in fits of giggles. When they had settled down again, they glanced back towards the distant cove where the two smugglers could be seen jumping up and down on the rocks in anger and shaking their fists wildly in the air. Amanda and Skelly also leapt up and down and waved their fists in the air, but for a wholly different reason – they were jumping for joy because they had escaped to safety.

In the meantime, the cabin cruiser was racing across the waves and Amanda had no idea how to slow it down. It had already left the smugglers' cove far behind them and was rapidly speeding around the cliffs to where the beach – from whence Amanda and Skelly had originally set off from earlier that afternoon – now loomed ahead.

"I don't know how to stop this thing, so I'm going to ram it into the sand," Amanda told Skelly. "That should slow us down... Brace yourself for a rough landing."

It was late evening by this time and there was only a small group of people left on the beach, who stared in astonishment at the speeding cabin cruiser that was approaching at a fair rate of knots. Amongst those people in the group were Amanda's parents, who had been scouring the shore for several hours whilst they searched for their missing daughter. The local police and the national coastguard had also been called in to help with their search, and Amanda's parents were busy talking to a police officer when the cabin cruiser suddenly appeared from around the headland to plough into the sand.

"What the blazes is going on?" said the police officer.

"I don't know," Amanda's father answered, "but my advice would be to *RUN!*"

It was lucky that they did run because everyone was forced to dive left, right and centre as the cabin cruiser skimmed through the middle of the gathered crowd, until it finally ground to a halt after digging itself into a deep furrow on the beach.

"I'm going to give that maniac a piece of my mind," raved Amanda's mother as she picked herself up and brushed the sand from her face and hair. But as she started towards the stricken vessel Amanda leapt from the deck with her backpack strapped to her.

"Hi Mummy, hi Daddy," she shouted as if nothing had happened; and then she ran to greet them, grinning from ear to ear.

For once in her life Mum was speechless, so Amanda's father took control of the situation.

"We've been extremely worried about you Amanda," he said. "We're very pleased to see that you are safe and well but I think you've got some serious explaining to do young lady."

Amanda thus commenced to relate the story of the day's events, with her audience listening intently. Naturally, she left Skelly out of the story because she knew that she could not reveal his identity. The police officer in charge of the investigation was called Inspector Sample and he was a very understanding man who waited patiently until Amanda's full story had unfolded. Then he walked over to the cabin cruiser to begin his investigation.

"Okay," he said, "let us find out exactly what is in these crates."

He took out a crowbar and prized open one of the lids, to discover that the crate was packed full of DVDs and computer games. Next, he opened another crate, and another, all with the same result.

"Aha! Just as I suspected," exclaimed Inspector Sample as he produced a walkie-talkie from an inside pocket of his tunic.Then, after a brief conversation with someone on the other end, he turned to speak to Amanda.

"The coastguard will now go and pick up the smugglers and their accomplices," he announced with a satisfied grin on his face. "We've been tracking these thugs for some time now and you've helped us out immensely. This gang has been smuggling pirate goods into the country and they've proved very difficult to catch, so there is a big reward on offer for their capture. I suggest that you go home now and get a good night's sleep. I will come by your cottage tomorrow morning to see you. Until then, I bid thee goodnight."

Amanda lay awake in bed that night. She felt tired out, but she was also pumped full of adrenalin after the day's adventure.

"I wonder what the reward will be for capturing those smugglers," she said to Skelly.

But Skelly failed to reply because he was not listening. Instead, he was sat upon the windowsill looking longingly at the starry sky. Amanda could tell that he was lost in a world of his own and she had a slight inkling as to what he was thinking.

"If I could choose my own reward Skelly, it would be to send you back to your home planet of Laktose so that you can be with your own family – and one day it will happen, just you wait and see."

However, she dropped off to sleep after saying this and dreamt about lots of nice things that she would be able to buy with her reward money.

CHAPTER ELEVEN

Skelly the Performing Seal

At ten o'clock the next morning there was a knock at the front door of the holiday cottage where the James family were staying. It turned out to be Inspector Sample at the door, who had called around to give Amanda her reward as promised; but first he told them all how happy everyone was with their results from the previous day and he thanked Amanda on behalf of the police force and the local townsfolk. Then came the news that Amanda was really waiting for.

"As a token of our appreciation," said Inspector Sample, "the entertainment manufacturer, whose goods we recovered, would like to give you two dozen DVDs or computer games of your choice."

Amanda drew a sharp intake of breath and all she could say was "Wow!" Inspector Sample paused his conversation to smile broadly at her before continuing with the second part of his congratulatory speech.

"On top of that, we – the police force, that is – would like to give you one hundred pounds to spend on whatever you choose to spend it on."

The speechless girl simply gazed at the Inspector in complete awe.

"And, finally, here are some complimentary tickets for you and your parents to go and see the circus that is currently in town. If you go before the performance starts you will also get to take a look behind the scenes... How does all that sound to you?"

Somehow or other Amanda managed to thank the Inspector although she felt a little tongue-tied.

"That's absolutely fantastic," she said. "Thank you."

"No, thank you young lady – you have done us a great service," he said, smiling broadly at her once again.

After that, the Inspector made his excuses and hurriedly departed because he said there was another important case urgently awaiting his attention.

"Aren't you the lucky one?" said Mum, when the Inspector had gone. "What are you going to do with all of that money?"

"I'm going to save it up for a special occasion," Amanda proudly replied. Then she ran upstairs to tell Skelly her great news.

Later that day the whole family went to the circus where, upon their arrival, they were warmly greeted by Ringo the ringmaster, who immediately took them on a guided tour behind the scenes. Amanda was first introduced to a family of trapeze artists known as The Great Tumbelinas, whom she really liked, and they invited her to watch them rehearse before the show began.

Next, it was time to meet the two clowns. Amanda was of the understanding that clowns were supposed to be funny but she thought these two men were not amusing in the slightest. In fact, they were two of the most miserable people whom she had ever met and this puzzled her because clowns were usually happy characters. She found their attitude to be most odd but she put it down to the fact that maybe they were just having a bad day, like everyone is entitled to at times.

During the afternoon Amanda met all manner of people including jugglers, fire-eaters, bareback horse riders and people on stilts, which left her with the opinion that if you wanted to see the weird and the wonderful then the circus was definitely the place to be.

However, as much as she enjoyed meeting many different artistes, best of all the animals were amongst Amanda's favourite things. There were tigers, lions, chimpanzees, prancing horses, dogs that jumped through hoops, elephants that stood up on their hind legs, a dancing bear, and – last but not least – a performing seal. She was totally enthralled by the whole experience and eagerly awaited the start of the show.

Naturally, Amanda had taken Skelly with her in his now familiar disguise as a backpack and whilst she and her family watched the lion tamer – Mr Claude Bottom – training his pets, Skelly clung tightly to Amanda's back and observed what was going on around him. He noticed that the performing seal seemed very sad and, using his powers of thought-speech, in seal language he asked her what was wrong.

"Oh dear," said the rather well-spoken seal, "I don't feel at all well and I'm not sure if I can go through with tonight's show, but I don't want to disappoint the girls and boys who will be in the audience."

"I have to admit that you do look a little pale," Skelly agreed.

"Oh no, I'm supposed to be this colour. You see, I'm a rare albino seal from Antarctica and my species has a tendency to suffer from the flu in warmer climates."

"I see," said Skelly. "I'm sorry that you don't feel very well and if there's anything that I can do to help you out please let me know."

"To be quite honest, I don't believe that you can be of any

assistance really, but thank you for offering all the same," Selina replied.

Skelly spent the next few moments deep in thought and then he came up with an idea.

"Perhaps I could stand in for you tonight," he suggested.

The seal tried to laugh but she ended up sneezing instead.

"I think that people might notice the difference between you and me," spluttered the seal, "because you don't really look much like a seal do you?"

"No, but I can change shape and I'm sure that I could imitate you perfectly," Skelly replied. "Would you like me to give it a try?"

"Oh, how very decent of you... Would you mind awfully? That would be a great burden off my shoulders."

"What do I have to do?" asked Skelly.

"Well, you have to be able to juggle, and be capable of balancing a ball on your nose also, and clap like a seal does with one's flippers. You know... the usual kind of stuff."

"I'm sure I can do all of those things," said Skelly, even though he had never tried doing any of them before. "I'll see you later."

"Before you go, there is one other thing that you have to do, and that's..."

But before the seal could finish what she was saying Amanda walked away with her backpack because it was time to go and watch The Great Tumbelinas rehearsing for their act.

When the time came for the evening performance to begin, Amanda and her parents were given ringside seats next to the entrance where all of the performers came in. Very soon the big top began to fill up with people and Amanda watched the crowd pour in. To her surprise, she saw Inspector Sample arrive and then watched him take a seat on the opposite side of the entrance to her. As soon as she spotted him she jumped out of her seat and waved hard to attract his attention, but although the Inspector noticed her he deliberately seemed to ignore her presence and buried his head deep into a copy of the schedule of events. Amanda thought his behaviour was very odd considering that he had been so nice to her earlier in the day; however, she thought it possible that he simply did not recognise her.

Before she could think any more about this matter, all of a sudden, with a loud fanfare and a roll of drums, Ringo the ringmaster announced the start of the show. Three prancing horses and three performing dogs raced into the arena straight away whilst their trainers rode bareback and carried out acrobatic manoeuvres, at the same time holding burning hoops of fire in their hands which the dogs jumped through.

Next came the clowns, and they were still not funny as far as Amanda could tell. Even the ringmaster seemed surprised by their act, for he was standing in the entrance near to where Amanda was seated and she could hear him asking the clowns what part of their act they were performing because it was not on his schedule. When the clowns left the arena there was very little applause from the audience, and Amanda then overheard Ringo telling them they were fired from the job because he thought they were so bad. After that, several acts came and went and then the ringmaster made a further announcement.

"Ladiees and Genteelmen," he bellowed in a slow, drawling sort of voice, "please put your flippers together for Selina the Performing Seal."

The audience laughed politely at his light-hearted patter and then they began to clap heartily as, right on cue, Skelly slipped out of sight of the audience by climbing down behind the stands and then re-entered via the main entrance in the form of Selina the Performing Seal.

Skelly's act was faultless. He began with a juggling display, using fish instead of clubs or balls, while at the same time skilfully balancing a beach ball upon his nose. Next, he flicked the ball from his tail to his flippers and headed it high into the air before catching it on his tail whilst standing on his head. The crowd went wild with delight and Skelly lapped-up all of the attention with gusto. Once again, the ringmaster seemed surprised by the act for it too had altered from his schedule; however, because the act was so good he congratulated Skelly enthusiastically as he left the arena.

The highlight of the show for Amanda came in the form of the trapeze artists and she watched in awe as they performed high-flying gymnastics several feet above the audience. The night seemed to slip by very quickly and, all too soon, Ringo the ringmaster made his final announcement.

"Ladiees and Genteelmen... and now it's time for the Grand Finale, the moment you have all been waiting for, when Selina the Performing Seal will now attempt a death-defying feat..."

Suddenly Skelly's ears began to prick up.

"She will be fired from this very cannon," Ringo continued, "whereupon she will hurtle forty feet into the air and be caught by two of the trapeze artists."

With his index finger, the ringmaster first pointed to a shiny black cannon and then towards the roof of the big top as he explained the scenario. Before he was allowed to continue there was a huge sigh of "Oooh!" and "Aaah!" from the audience as they looked at the cannon and then peered towards the faraway roof of the big top. In the meantime, Skelly was beginning to feel terribly sick.

"Uh-oh!" he muttered under his breath. "This bit wasn't in the script." And then he suddenly recalled that Selina had been trying to tell him there was more to the act but Amanda had walked away with him before the seal could finish what she was saying.

"And, after that..." the ringmaster went on.

"*What? There's more?!!*" murmured a panic-stricken Skelly.

"...Selina the Performing Seal will be placed on this bicycle and sent along a tightrope from where she will then fall into the safety net far beneath her," exclaimed the ringmaster with a broad grin slowly spreading across his face.

Whilst he watched the bicycle being hoisted high up towards the roof of the big top, Skelly prepared himself for the finale that would probably end all finales which was to be his moment of glory. He was absolutely petrified but he had promised Selina that he would stand in for her and, not being one for backing out, quaking like a blancmange he bravely wobbled onto the main rostrum where the cannon was situated.

He was then lifted upwards in a giant sling where he remained suspended in mid-air, swinging above the barrel of the cannon for what seemed like an eternity, whilst the lights were dimmed and the drums began to roll. Finally, he was lowered into the dark mouth of the cannon and Ringo the ringmaster struck a giant match.

There then followed a fizzing and crackling sound, that was amplified ten-fold inside the barrel of the big black gun, before an almighty flash and a thunderous roar sent Skelly rocketing into the air. The pyrotechnics were purely for show, of course, because there was actually a springboard inside the barrel of the cannon that launched Skelly into space, which the ringmaster operated by a secret lever whilst the gunpowder ignited.

Not surprisingly, Skelly was a lot lighter than the blubbery mass of Selina the genuine seal; therefore, he shot across the big top faster than he would have done if he had been heavier. Split-second timing was crucial on the part of the acrobats but, because he was travelling so fast, they simply could not catch him. There was a look of astonishment on the acrobats' faces as he flew above their heads, but nowhere near such a look of astonishment as there was on Skelly's face when he collided with the canvas roof of the big top!

The springy material expanded outwards as it slowed him down but when it reached its maximum stretching point he rebounded and was swiftly catapulted downwards. Skelly did indeed make contact with the saddle of the bicycle, but much harder than was intended, and with such impetus that the bicycle careered along the tightrope at a zillion miles per hour. The unfortunate alien managed to grab the handlebars to steady himself as he fell off the tightrope, and he was still hanging on to the bicycle for dear life when he hit the safety net. He then bounced back into the air to be flung clean through the main entrance of the arena. The audience thought this was all part of the act of course and, by this time, they were on their feet for a standing ovation with deafening applause.

After Skelly had disappeared through the entrance Amanda had leapt to her feet, as did Inspector Sample, and, accompanied by three well-built policemen, as fast as scattering silverfish they had been the first out of the main arena. Amanda was hot on their heels because she was deeply concerned for her little friend. Once they had all disappeared through the canvas flap that served as the main entrance to the big top, a horrible groaning sound could be heard and Amanda feared the worse for Skelly's well-being. But her fears were quickly allayed because Skelly had received a soft landing when he had collided with the two awful circus clowns.

"I am arresting you in the name of the law," Amanda heard Inspector Sample say, and once again she became worried.

"Oh no, what was Skelly supposed to have done?" she asked herself, but then she realised that the Inspector was talking to the clowns.

After making his arrest, Inspector Sample turned to speak to Amanda.

"I need to have a chat with you in a little while young miss," he said quite sternly. But, when he realised that Amanda seemed extremely worried by what he had just said, he gave her a reassuring smile.

"Don't worry; it's all good news, I can assure you," he added.

At that moment Ringo the ringmaster appeared with a concerned frown upon his face too. Inspector Sample explained to him the reason why he had arrested the two clowns and, having satisfied himself that his star attraction was not injured in any way, he then spoke to the seal.

"I am so pleased that you are okay Selina. Everybody in the audience is asking for an encore but I think that you've had enough for one day so you had better come back into the arena and take a big bow instead."

Then the ringmaster turned around to address Amanda.

"My dear, would you mind coming into the arena with Selina also?" he said. "After all, you are a star in your own right too you know."

Amanda did not know exactly what the ringmaster had meant

about her being a star but she willingly obliged with the task of helping Skelly the seal back to the main arena. After their re-emergence there followed several minutes of rapturous applause before the ringmaster eventually raised his hands and complete silence reigned all around.

"Ladiees and Genteelmen," he said in his customary manner, "there have been some strange happenings here tonight and to explain the situation I would like to present Inspector Sample from forensics."

The Inspector took the microphone and went on to explain to everyone that the two clowns were in fact pick-pockets who had robbed several members of the audience, unbeknownst to them, while they were watching the show. The real clowns had been drugged and then tied up in their caravans while the two impostors had taken their place. However, the ringmaster's suspicions had been aroused that something was not quite right with the clowns so he alerted the police. Fortunately, Inspector Sample and his men were in the audience and a secret investigation was launched but they were waiting for Amanda to make a sudden move before acting. As a result, the two pick-pockets would now spend a long time under lock and key for their crimes and everyone who had been robbed would have their belongings returned to them.

The audience then learned that, if it had not been for Amanda, the Inspector would not have even been there but, after the previous day's seaside escapade, he had a hunch that he would capture more villains if he followed the young girl around. Inspector Sample finished his speech by thanking Amanda for her help in bringing the crooked clowns to justice and then he presented her with a further reward of one hundred pounds.

Following on from the Inspector's speech, The Great Tumbelinas handed a large bouquet of flowers to Amanda, together with free tickets which would allow her entry to any of their circus performances at any venue in the country. Ringo the ringmaster rounded off the evening by asking the audience to give Amanda three big cheers, after which she was permitted to have the final word when he unexpectedly handed her the microphone.

Firstly, she told everyone that she was overwhelmed with their generosity and, secondly, Amanda said that when she grew up she would like to be a famous trapeze artiste just like The Great Tumbelinas were. Then she curtsied politely before leaving the ring to her own standing ovation.

What an adventurous couple of days it had been for Amanda and Skelly and a holiday neither of them would ever forget.

CHAPTER TWELVE

Amanda Meets Mr Peabody

One particularly warm midsummer evening, a visitor – whose name was Miss Peabody – dropped in to see Amanda's mother. Miss Peabody was a spinster who lived with her father in a delightful thatched cottage in the village and she was the president of the Darwood Women's Guild: this was a village association which Amanda's mum had recently joined because she had become quite involved with community activities around the local area over the summer months.

Amanda heard the crunching of gravel beneath the tyres of Miss Peabody's car as she drew up outside the house and she went over to her bedroom window just to be nosey. She watched Miss Peabody get out of the car and noticed that she was not alone, for there was another person sitting in the front passenger seat. Once Miss Peabody had disappeared into the house with Amanda's mum the passenger then got out of the car.

This passenger turned out to be an old man who was dressed in a light-coloured suit and wore a tatty-looking straw hat. In his left hand he held a wooden cane – that was a walking stick as far as Amanda could tell. As soon as he was out of the car the man put his hand into his jacket pocket and fished out a pipe, which he stuffed with tobacco and thrust into his mouth before lighting it.

For quite a while Amanda watched the old man with some curiosity because he seemed to be very interested in the barn which was currently undergoing renovation. After studying the building at great length whilst he puffed away on his pipe the old man eventually began to walk towards it. At this point Amanda realised the cane served its purpose more as an ornament than a necessity because the man actually walked at quite a brisk pace, with the cane slung over his shoulder in such a way that a soldier would carry a rifle. When the man got to the barn he went around the back of the building and disappeared from view, so Amanda thought she would go outside to find out exactly what he was up to.

A few minutes later she found him snooping around inside the barn and decided to confront him. She cleared her throat in order to get his attention because she did not want to startle him, but he appeared not to hear her, so Amanda walked around the perimeter of the barn's inner wall until the old man finally caught sight of her.

"I'm Amanda," she said.

The old man merely stared at her, saying not a word.

"What are you doing here?" she asked.

"Reminiscing," he replied in a kindly, gentle sounding voice. "What about you... what are you doing here?"

"I live here!" Amanda said in a surprised voice as if the old man should have known that already.

An awkward silence then followed.

"What does reminiscing mean?" she eventually asked.

"Looking back... at some good times that have long since passed me by."

"Oh, I understand," she answered, but she still seemed puzzled all the same.

The old man took a long draw on his pipe and then blew out a cloud of blue smoke which filled the air inside the barn. This did not bother Amanda in the slightest because she did not find the pipe smoke to be at all repulsive as so many people do; in fact, she thought that it had quite a sweet aroma of vanilla about it.

"Used to play in here when I was a kid," the old man said between puffs.

"Really? Was that a long time ago?"

"Probably before your own parents were even a twinkle in their parents' eyes," the old man replied with a smile on his face.

Amanda smiled back, although she had not quite worked out what he meant.

"Used to live in the big house myself you see lass. I bet it's changed a bit since my day though. And this old barn is becoming more modernised I notice."

"Yes, it's going to be my stable," Amanda proudly stated.

"I got banned from being in here," the old man told her.

"Me too," giggled Amanda.

All of a sudden he seemed to become down in the dumps.

"I was sent away not long after that," he continued. "It wasn't really my parents' fault... it was the darn doctors'. Said I was mad they did, and my parents believed them – that's the ridiculous thing – so they sent me away. That was how it was in those days, see."

"Why did they think you were mad?" Amanda asked.

"Well..." began the old man, and then he hesitated. "Can you keep a secret?"

Amanda nodded her head.

"Yes, I'm good at keeping secrets," she said. "I've got some of my own too."

His gaze penetrated hers for a moment or two and Amanda noticed that his eyes were brown and full of trust – just like a small puppy's she thought.

"Okay," he eventually said, "then I shall tell you my secret."

But before he had a chance to say another word Miss Peabody called out his name.

"Father," she shouted. "Father... Where are you?"

Her voice sounded full of anxiety.

"Tsk!" tutted the old man. "Typical isn't it? I make a new friend and I have to go before we are properly acquainted."

Feeling bitterly disappointed that he had to go, Amanda agreed with him.

"She worries about me so much, you know. Just because I'm getting on in years she thinks I can't look after myself. Nags me to death she does. Daughters, eh! Well, it has been a pleasure to meet you lass and I shall look forward to telling you my secret some other time perhaps."

"*FATHER!*" Miss Peabody's voice interrupted again, and she was beginning to sound frantic.

"Coming dear..."

The old man slipped his pipe back into his jacket pocket and strode from the barn, tapping the ground with his walking cane every three paces or so as he went.

"I've been so worried about you father," Amanda heard Miss Peabody say. "Where have you been?"

"I've been for a leak behind the barn," joked the old man.

"Oh, father! How could you? Especially when we are visiting someone... I feel so ashamed."

As she heard the car doors slam shut, Amanda sniggered heartily at the old man's successful attempt to wind up his daughter. Then there was the sound of crunching gravel as Miss Peabody drove away. Amanda had really enjoyed meeting Mr Peabody and hoped upon hope that she would meet him again some day soon, and maybe she would then find out what his secret was.

Approximately one week after Mr Peabody's visit Amanda returned home from school to find her mother in a rather flustered state.

"What's the matter Mum?" she asked.

"Oh, dear," Mum replied, "I have a bit of a dilemma on my hands because I have volunteered to arrange the flowers in the village church on behalf of the Women's Guild ready for a special church service on Wednesday, but I hadn't realised that your father has an important convention to attend tonight and he won't be home until late."

Amanda could not understand why this was such a major catastrophe in her mother's life, so she enquired as to exactly what the problem was.

"The problem is," Mum told her, "that I don't have a childminder to watch over you. I've telephoned everyone that I know and they are all busy this evening."

"Well, I suppose I could come along to the church with you," Amanda suggested.

"Oh, yes, what a good idea!" exclaimed Mum. "I had never given that a thought because I have been so stressed out. You can even help me and we'll get the job done twice as fast."

The rota for flower arranging at the church normally involved two members from the Women's Guild and that was exactly how it was to be on that particular evening, with her mother's associate being

Miss Peabody. And when they had finished arranging the flowers she invited them around for tea.

Upon arrival at the home of their guest Amanda and her mum were first given a guided tour of the house. Then they were treated to a wonderful supper which consisted of hot buttered toast with large dollops of fresh strawberry jam, followed by English muffins and freshly-brewed Indian tea. Afterwards, the conversation became boring for Amanda because the adults were talking mostly about flowers and cake-baking – the usual old fogey kind of stuff in her opinion – and so she asked Miss Peabody if she could take another look around the house. Miss Peabody had no objection to this request and Amanda set off to explore every nook and cranny.

The inside of the cottage was a treasure trove of antiquities from a bygone era that reminded Amanda of a miniature museum. She observed also that Miss Peabody obviously liked flowers, for there were vases full of chrysanthemums and hyacinths throughout the property that gave off a lovely scent. Amanda noticed that there was a strange kind of quietness about the cottage, which brought back memories of her own grandmother's house in London: from the clock on the kitchen wall that tick-tocked merrily to and fro, to the swishing sound that the rocking-chair made when she sat on it.

. All along the hallway were hung many pictures and photographs, some of which must have been very old, Amanda thought, because they were black and white prints. Whilst she gazed at the old pictures in turn, one of them suddenly caught her attention. It was a sketch signed with a name that she found impossible to read, and there was no doubt at all that it was an accurate drawing of Skelly!

As quick as could be, Amanda rushed into the living room and, at an appropriate moment, she interrupted the adults' conversation. The three females then went into the hallway where Amanda enquired about the sketch.

"Who drew this picture?" she asked in an excited voice.

"My father did," Miss Peabody proudly announced. Then she followed it up with a chuckle. "He drew that sketch when he was just a boy; he had quite a vivid imagination, didn't he? What a strange creature in the drawing... I can't imagine where he could get such an idea from."

"He's not a creature, he's a being," Amanda said.

"What do you mean by that?" asked her mother and Miss Peabody in perfect harmony because they did not understand what she meant.

"It's not important," Amanda replied, and she moved swiftly on to her next question. "What is your father's first name?"

"*Amanda!*" exclaimed her mother. "Don't be so nosey. Fancy asking Miss Peabody so many questions – It's very rude of you."

"Oh, it really isn't a problem," said Miss Peabody with a smile on her face. "I'm pleased that she is taking such an interest in my father... His name is Edward but he has always preferred to be called Ted."

Suddenly, Amanda's eyes lit up because she remembered Skelly had told her that Ted was the name of the boy who had once lived in their house and befriended him many years ago, and she was slowly putting two and two together.

"Is he here now?" asked Amanda rather excitedly.

"No, he has gone to visit an acquaintance for a few days but he'll be back at the weekend. I believe you have met him once before, so you must come by to visit him when you can; I'm sure he would love to see you again. Besides, it may do him some good to talk to someone of such a young age. He doesn't get out much any more and the poor old chap seems to be losing his marbles somewhat. Just lately, he has often mentioned an old friend of his whom he hasn't seen for years, and he has become rather depressed – it worries me quite a bit."

Amanda looked longingly at her mother.

"Please Mummy, can we come back at the weekend and see Mr Peabody?"

"Well, I don't see why not," Amanda's mum replied. "Would Saturday be okay with you Miss Peabody? I could bring those cake tins over that I promised you."

It was agreed that they would return on Saturday and, with this date arranged, Amanda and her mother went home. Amanda felt so excited that she could hardly wait to get home and tell Skelly the good news because, in her view, Ted Peabody had to be the person who had hidden Skelly's space-egg all those years ago. What, with having a drawing of Skelly in the house, and by a man called Ted, it was all too much to be a coincidence.

When Saturday came around, Amanda returned with her mother to visit Miss Peabody and her father. She had taken Skelly with her masquerading as a backpack as usual and, when they arrived at their cottage, she ran ahead of her mother to knock on the front door. This was met with a brief delay before Miss Peabody eventually answered the door and invited them in. Full of excited anticipation, Amanda peered around her host expecting to see Miss Peabody's father waiting to greet them but there was no sign of anyone else in the house. Miss Peabody noticed the look of disappointment on Amanda's face and seemed to know what she wanted.

"Come on in and I'll take you to meet my father," she said. He is in his bedroom where he spends a lot of time these days."

Amanda immediately cheered up.

"Oh, by the way, I forgot to mention when you were here the other evening that my father used to live in your house when he was a young boy," added Miss Peabody.

"Yes, I know," Amanda replied.

"How do you know?" asked Amanda's mother with a puzzled expression on her face.

"He told me when he came to our house with Miss Peabody."

"You must have had quite a chat," said Mum.

"We did, but we didn't get around to finishing our conversation," Amanda concluded as they mounted the stairs.

Miss Peabody rapped on the bedroom door and then hesitated before entering. They found Ted Peabody seated in an easy chair, gazing out of his bedroom window at the gently rolling pastures which surrounded the cottage.

"Father, I've brought Mrs James and her daughter Amanda to meet you..."

Ted Peabody did not answer his daughter.

"He's as deaf as a post you know," Miss Peabody apologised.

Then, in a much louder voice, she repeated his name.

"FATHER!"

The old man looked up, glancing first at Amanda and then at her mother, but with an apparent lack of interest he turned his head away and continued to stare out of the window.

"I am sorry," said Miss Peabody, "but it appears that today isn't one of his better days. I think we should go now and leave him to his thoughts."

Amanda felt extremely dismayed upon hearing this suggestion.

"Oh!" she said rather woefully. "Could I please stay here and talk to your father? Maybe I can cheer him up."

"If you wish," Miss Peabody replied, "but if he continues to ignore you, do come downstairs and you can help us in the kitchen – your mum and I will be doing a spot of baking."

Amanda stayed in the bedroom with the old man. She sat down on a chair and began to chatter nineteen-to-the-dozen about nothing in particular. After a short time, it became obvious to Amanda that Ted Peabody had no interest in her conversation, which she found strange considering that he had been quite friendly when they had previously met, so she decided to take the bull by the horns and be direct with the subject that she had really come to talk about.

"I know your secret Mr Peabody," Amanda boldly proclaimed.

The old man cast a sideways glance in her direction but still he said nothing.

"Well, it's not really a secret any more," she continued, "because I share it with you."

"What secret is that young lady?"

The old man had finally found his voice and, although his reply was a little snappy, Amanda still thought that it sounded gentle.

"Well, when I visited here just the other evening I was looking at the pictures in your hallway when I noticed the sketch that you had drawn when you were a boy," Amanda began.

Ted Peabody interrupted Amanda as he began to show a little more interest in what she was saying.

"Which sketch would that be?" he enquired. "There are several hanging in the hallway that I drew in my youth."

"I think you know the one that I mean – the picture of Skelly!"

All of a sudden, Ted Peabody's face became animated.

"*You know about Skelly?*" he asked in surprise.

"Yes," said Amanda. "I live with my parents in the same house that you used to live in many years ago, remember?"

"Yes of course I remember, but Skelly must have gone by now surely?

"No, Mr Peabody, he is still there."

The old man's facial expression suddenly changed, as if a great weight had been lifted from his shoulders.

"I knew that I hadn't imagined him... I just knew it!" he exclaimed.

"You thought that you had imagined Skelly?" Amanda said enquiringly.

"Yes, in a way. I was made to believe that he was a figment of my imagination. That's what I was trying to tell you about doctors when we last met; they convinced my parents that I was mad so I was sent away to a special school for kids who were supposed to be crazy. When I was eventually allowed out of that place I moved to another part of the country to try and get as far away as possible from it. I lived there for many years, got married and then my daughter was born. When my wife passed away, my daughter suggested that we move back to the village where I first grew up because I was always talking about it, apparently. She had never been here but she fell in love with Darwood as soon as she saw it and we moved back. I had been forced to shut him out of my head when I was younger but I never really forgot about Skelly you know."

Amanda truly believed what Ted Peabody was telling her because she had noticed how excited he had become when she mentioned his name.

"How can he still be here after all these years?" said the old man, partly to himself.

"Because he hasn't been able to return to his planet yet," Amanda explained.

"You haven't told anyone else about him have you?" he asked in a concerned voice.

"No, Mr Peabody, I daren't. That's why I'm talking to you, because he's our secret."

"Call me Ted."

"I'd rather call you Mr Peabody if you don't mind. Mum has always taught me to be polite to my elders and to address them correctly, and she would kill me is she heard me calling you by your first name because she would think I was being disrespectful."

"You have very good manners young lady and you are a credit to your mother."

"Thanks," Amanda said rather bashfully.

"May I suggest, therefore, that you call me Ted when we are out of earshot but address me as Mr Peabody when in the company of your mother?"

"That would work," Amanda said with a smile; she had known all along that the old fellow was a kind man.

"So, going back to our friend Skelly... How is he? Does he still look the same? Does he remember me? I suppose he must do or he wouldn't have told you about me. Oh, this is such a surprise... and what a great surprise it is too."

"I have another surprise for you," said Amanda, and then she paused.

Ted Peabody raised his eyebrows in anticipation.

"Skelly is here with me," she said. "Would you like to see him?"

The old man suddenly leapt from his armchair and began to search all around him.

"Skelly is here in this room? Where is he, I can't see him?"

At that very instant there was a popping sound and Skelly transformed from his backpack shape into his normal form. After staring at each other for a few moments with tears in their eyes Skelly and Ted embraced each other fondly, just like long-lost friends would do – which is exactly what they were, of course – and, for the time being, Amanda had been forgotten. She decided that it was time for her to leave the room so that Skelly and Ted could talk about old times; after all, they had a lot to catch up on.

A short while later – which seemed like an age to Amanda – Ted called her back to his room and the trio talked and laughed about adventures old and new. Then Amanda became serious.

"Mr Peabody... sorry, I mean Ted... I really need to ask you about something that is very important."

"Fire away young lady," Ted replied with a new vitality about his voice.

"Can you remember what you did with Skelly's space-egg?"

"Oh, my goodness!" exclaimed Ted. "I had completely forgotten about that. I recall taking the space-egg away and hiding it somewhere but I can't quite remember where. Now, let me think..."

Amanda and Skelly waited anxiously as Ted paced around his bedroom with his hand on his temple as he attempted to rack his brain. Suddenly, he stopped in his tracks and clicked his fingers in the air.

"I've got it!" he exclaimed. "I have just remembered where I buried it."

"*You buried it?*" said Amanda and Skelly together.

"Yes," said Ted. "I thought it was a good idea at the time, but maybe it wasn't such a good one after all because it will probably be a rusty pile of junk by now."

"On the contrary," Skelly told him. "My space-egg will actually be in perfect condition because it is made from materials which are unknown to mankind and they don't corrode."

"That's fantastic news," said Amanda, "but you still haven't told us where you buried the space-egg Ted."

"I buried it at my old house – where you live now of course – in the disused vegetable plot that was once the Victorian kitchen garden. I do hope that it is still there."

Before the conversation could go any further, approaching footsteps could suddenly be heard on the landing.

"Someone's coming," warned Amanda. "Change shape Skelly, and make it snappy!"

No sooner had Skelly changed shape when there was a light rap on the door and then Miss Peabody poked her head inside the bedroom.

"Your mother says that it is time for you to leave now Amanda because she has a lot to do this afternoon," she said.

Amanda stood up to say farewell to Ted Peabody. He then threw his arms around her to give both her and the backpack a great big hug at the same time.

"Do call again to see me, won't you?" said Ted. "This afternoon has been an absolute pleasure… thank you!"

For a moment or two Miss Peabody stood and stared at her father in astonishment. Then, as she walked with Amanda to the front door, she commented on what she had just seen.

"I don't know what you have done to my father but, whatever it was, you have made him look fifty years younger. It's the happiest I have seen him for a long time, so please take him up on his offer and come to visit again very soon; the presence of your company seems to have done him the power of good."

Amanda confirmed that she would return as soon as possible, and she thanked Miss Peabody for what had been a wonderful day out.

CHAPTER THIRTEEN

A Lucky Find

The remainder of the summer holidays went by so fast that, before Amanda knew what was happening, the time came to return to school for the beginning of the autumn term. She had many stories to tell, and her classmates listened intently as she related the numerous tales of her summer adventures, although it was with great difficulty that she managed not to mention Skelly's name. Her stories were a good start to the new term because her teacher, Miss Throwpee, awarded Amanda with three gold stars for each written essay and this immediately placed her at the top of her class.

During another lesson on that first day back at school, Miss Devent, the history teacher, announced that there would be a forthcoming day trip to a local museum. History was one of Amanda's favourite subjects; therefore, she instantly put her name down for this trip and looked forward to the day out immensely. With so much going on, that first day of term passed by really quickly and it was soon time to go home.

When Amanda arrived back at her home she found her father hard at work in the old kitchen garden. He had taken a day's leave from his job and had decided to loosen the soil in order to plant some vegetable seeds so that they would be fully-grown in time for the winter months. This is just what Amanda had been waiting for and she sat down on the lawn, placing her backpack on the ground beside her, so that she and Skelly could watch her father and witness the very moment that Skelly's long-lost space-egg was unearthed. Full of hope, they watched patiently for about an hour until Amanda's father eventually stopped what he was doing and walked across his vegetable patch to talk to her.

"Don't you have anything to do?" he asked. "You must be very bored sitting there just watching me work."

"It's quite interesting actually," Amanda replied. "You never know what you might find."

"I can assure you that there is nothing here but soil and roots," said Dad. "I don't think for one minute that I shall dig up any buried treasure!"

Amanda laughed at that.

"I don't think you will find any treasure either Dad, but I'll just sit here anyway – I'm really having fun," Amanda said, and she smiled innocently at him.

"Whatever you wish," said her father, giving his shoulders a shrug, and then he re-started his Rotavator.

He ploughed deep into the ground, breaking up the surface with the large blades and turning over the soil as he went, until he suddenly struck an object and, with a noisy clanging sound, the Rotavator momentarily leapt into the air. Then Amanda stood up and held her breath as her father began to dig the ground with his spade, whilst he tried to uncover whatever the hidden object was below the surface. After a short time the object was exposed and Amanda's tension turned out to be unnecessary because her father had uncovered nothing more than a large lump of rock.

By late evening Amanda's dad had put away his Rotavator and started to sew his vegetable seeds. There was clearly nothing to be found in the old vegetable patch, so a rather disappointed Amanda retired to the house with her equally forlorn companion. She began to think that maybe Ted had been wrong and he had not buried Skelly's space-egg in the vegetable plot – after all, several years had passed by and Miss Peabody did warn her that the old man was losing his marbles. Perhaps it was actually buried somewhere else in the grounds of the house and Ted had simply got it wrong. It was a huge garden and Amanda had not got a clue where to start looking, so she was concerned that the missing space-egg may never be located.

When Monday morning came around, it was the day of the school trip. As was now customary, Amanda took her rabbit-featured backpack with her almost everywhere that she went, and today was no different because Skelly was going to visit the museum with her.

The museum was located in a huge complex and there was so much to see that Amanda knew she was going to be in for a great day out. But, little did she know, that she would discover far more than she had bargained for.

The tour of the museum started with the ice age period, where woolly mammoths had been rebuilt from remains that had been recovered locally. Then there was a field trip to the site of a neighbouring Roman villa, where Amanda learned how people used to live during Roman times, and she marvelled at the innovations that were used all those centuries ago.

Next on the list came a Viking discovery centre, and then a mediaeval village reconstruction. In fact, all ages throughout history were covered by this one museum: from the Tudor period to the

Elizabethan era, from Victorian to Edwardian, every period was represented; and there was a modern history section too, which incorporated recent wartime artefacts.

Whilst Amanda was viewing the Second World War exhibits in the modern history area, she suddenly felt a sharp pain in her side when Skelly dug her in the ribs with one of his bony fingers.

"Stop that!" she snapped.

Her nearby classmates simply stared at her in bewilderment as if she was going mad.

"Who are you talking to?" asked her best friend, Clare.

"Nobody," Amanda replied and, although she smiled sweetly at her, she could feel her cheeks flush.

Then Skelly dug Amanda in the ribs again.

"Ouch!" she yelled.

She shouted this so loudly that everyone in the hall heard her and they all stopped to stare.

"Are you alright Amanda?" asked Miss Devent with a worried frown on her face.

"Yes I'm fine thank you Miss... Can I go to the loo please?"

"Of course you can. It's over there," Miss Devent said, pointing across the hall.

Amanda hurriedly rushed over to the public toilets where, after she had checked out all of the cubicles to make sure that they were alone, she had words with her annoying little friend.

"What on Earth is the matter with you Skelly? That dig in the ribs really hurt me."

"I'm sorry," Skelly apologised in an excited voice, "but I had to get your attention somehow or other because I have just spotted my space-egg!"

"Don't be so ridiculous," Amanda said. "How could it possibly be in here, this is a museum?"

"It's definitely there," Skelly said.

He said this so convincingly that Amanda finally began to believe him.

"Are you sure?" she asked.

"Positive."

"Then where have you seen it?"

"Hanging on the wall in the main hall," he exclaimed.

"But that's impossible," said Amanda. "This is the World War Two section, so what would it be doing in there?"

"I don't know!" Skelly argued. "I tell you, my space-egg is definitely here; there is no doubt about it. Let me show you when we go back into the hall. I'll dig you in the ribs again when we are near to it."

"Oh, very well then," Amanda agreed, "but don't you dare poke your finger into my side so hard this time or I'll slap you".

They returned to the exhibition hall after that, and, when Amanda was in the right spot, she received yet another swift dig in her ribs that hurt just as much as it had done on the previous occasion. Amanda scowled at Skelly, who was slung loosely over her left shoulder; then she immediately lashed out at her backpack, which obviously caught the attention of her schoolmates once again.

"There was a spider on my backpack," she told them all, "and I was trying to swat it away."

Her pathetic fib seemed to be accepted by everyone and they returned to whatever they were doing, whilst Amanda's attention had now been drawn to an object situated on the wall before her, which did not resemble her idea of what she thought Skelly's space-egg would look like in the slightest. In fact, the object was just like all of the others from that era, with the appearance of being dull and drab-looking and, more often than not, covered in camouflage paint in order to blend in with their surroundings. However, Amanda read the inscription that accompanied the egg-shaped object with great interest.

ORIGIN UNKNOWN

"This particular specimen was discovered in the kitchen garden of a house in a nearby village and it is believed to be an unexploded bomb. It is the only example of such an object found to exist throughout the entire world, thus making it a suspected secret weapon. Tests were carried out to explode the device in a controlled environment but it proved to be indestructible and was therefore deemed to be perfectly harmless. Further tests revealed nothing else, except that the device is constructed from a material unknown to mankind. No country has ever laid claim to this object nor has any government ever admitted to know the inventor of this secret weapon, therefore the device is a unique and priceless artefact."

After reading this inscription Amanda was flabbergasted. It appeared that Ted Peabody had been right all along, for Skelly was adamant that this was his missing space-egg which had indeed been buried in the old vegetable plot in the grounds of their house, until a later occupant had uncovered it at some time before donating it to the museum. For the remainder of the day, and when she went to bed that night, the space-egg was at the forefront of Amanda's thoughts. But, now that she and Skelly had located it, the next question was going to be, how would they get it out of the museum?

She decided that the best solution would be to enlist the help of Ted Peabody because he was the only person who shared the secret of Skelly's existence on Earth and he apparently had contacts with people in high places. Getting to see Ted was no longer a major problem because, now that he knew his friend Skelly was still around, he often turned up when Miss Peabody came to visit Amanda's mum; then the three of them would meet inside the old barn and just have fun passing the time of day. So, Amanda made up her mind that next time she saw Ted she would ask him for some advice.

CHAPTER FOURTEEN

Amanda's Winter Wonderland

Autumn soon turned into winter and this brought with it shorter daylight hours and colder weather. By this time of year the countryside had already become quite bare because, during the autumn months, many trees had shed their leaves and there were precious few flowers – if any at all – left in bloom. The mornings were cold and frosty too, with Jack Frost spreading his icy fingers to turn all that he touched into artistically sculpted patterns of white.

Every day Amanda looked longingly up to the sky, searching for signs of snow. She loved snow; it was cold and wet but it was so beautiful to look at and great fun to play in. Her dream finally came true in early December when the first snow of winter fell on a Tuesday morning. She awoke later than usual on that day, feeling all cosy and warm in her snug little bed and rather reluctant to go to school. When she pulled back her curtains she could not believe what she saw because it was a complete white-out, with the entire landscape fully-carpeted in a thick, white blanket of virgin snow. This was a fantastic sight to behold, and when the snow fell in such large quantities there was also an added bonus that there would be an extra day off school.

Amanda hurriedly got dressed and raced downstairs for breakfast. On cold winter mornings her mother always made porridge so that she had something warm in her stomach to start the day, and she wolfed down her porridge in record time because she could hardly wait to get outside and play in the snow. After she had eaten, Amanda donned her Wellington boots and then she put on her warm, waterproof snowsuit before telling her parents that she was going outside.

As she stepped out of the front door the cold air almost took her breath away; however, she quickly became used to it and the temperature became the furthest thought in her mind. It turned out that Skelly did not feel the cold at all because of his thick jelly-like flesh which insulated him. Nevertheless, Amanda had made him wear a woolly hat and scarf, just in case.

The snow was knee-deep and Amanda immediately set to work building a snowman on her front lawn. When she had finished her work of art the snowman stood nearly six feet high, and for a finishing touch she added a carrot to give it a nose and used lumps of coal for the eyes. On Skelly's advice she found smaller pieces of coal to give it a smiley mouth and went hunting for some appropriately-shaped twigs to form the arms and hands. Then she stood back so that she and Skelly could admire the finished product. Satisfied that her snow sculpture could not be improved upon, and with this task now complete, Amanda asked her parents for their permission to let her go sledging.

"But you don't have a toboggan," said Amanda's mother.

"I know," was her reply. "I can just watch everyone else having fun though."

"Very well then," Mum agreed, "but make sure that you are back at home for lunch two hours from now, or I shall be very annoyed with you."

Full of the joys of winter, Amanda set off along the lane, trudging through the deep snow and leaving huge footprints behind her as she went. Just around the corner from where she lived there was a small mound known as Primrose Hill and, when she got there, she found that several of her school chums were already making the most of their snow day. While she watched the children playing and having such great fun, Amanda mentioned to Skelly how she wished that she had a toboggan too. So, from a safe distance where they could not be seen, Skelly nipped behind a large oak tree and willingly obliged her wish by transforming himself into a fine-looking toboggan.

Being that he was so small, Skelly was only very light and Amanda easily carried him to the top of the hill, where she placed him down on the snow and climbed aboard. Then, digging her feet into the snow, she kicked-off and launched herself down the slippery slope, holding on tightly to Skelly's ears in order to give her some support.

Skelly had observed the other toboggans for some time and he had moulded his body into a shape that was far more aerodynamic than the rest, which made him the fastest toboggan on the run. This quickly became noticeable to the other children and, very soon, they gathered around to admire Amanda's new toy. Amongst these children was Terry Bull, the school bully.

"Hey Mandy, that's a nice sled," he remarked. "Can I have a look at it please?"

Although he had addressed her by the shortened form of her name that she did not really care for, Amanda thought how polite Terry had been and that maybe he had turned over a new leaf since his classroom outburst. Therefore, she consented to his request without holding any grudge towards him for his previous bad behaviour.

"Yes, certainly, of course you can have a look," she replied.

"Where did you get this?" asked Terry. "I've never seen a toboggan as cool as yours before."

"A friend of mine made it for me," was the best reply she could think of without telling a whopper.

"Can I have a go?" Terry asked with a pleasant smile on his face.

"No," said Amanda, rather abruptly. "I'm sorry but I can't let you have a go because I promised my friend that I would look after it and that it would not come to any harm."

"What do you mean, NO?" said Terry, suddenly becoming angry.

His smile had completely vanished, while his expression had turned into a look of rage. Before Amanda had a chance to reply, Terry gave her a hefty shove, which made her fall off her toboggan and into the snow. Then his friends held her down whilst Terry jumped onto the toboggan and took off. Amanda was very upset.

"Hey, that's mine – Give it back!" she cried, but Terry was already halfway down the hillside.

When he returned to the top of the hill for a second run, Amanda tried to grab her toboggan away from him but her efforts were thwarted when she was instantly bombarded with snowballs by Terry Bull's friends, forcing her to retreat in terror. Meanwhile, Skelly was at the mercy of the bully whom he had dealt with once before and he hated to see Amanda so upset, so he came up with a plan to get even again.

"Right, that does it!' he said to himself when Terry kicked-off for the second time. "I'm going to teach this monkey a lesson that he will never forget."

So, when they were more than halfway down the hill, Skelly suddenly changed direction, which made Terry Bull realise that he was no longer in control of the situation.

"Hey! What's happening?" Terry yelled in alarm.

Skelly had deliberately steered in another direction because he had spotted a tree stump, virtually buried in the snow, and he was now heading directly for it. Then, at the very instant when Skelly collided with the tree stump, Terry was thrown from the toboggan and flung into the air. At the foot of the hill there was a large pond, which was completely frozen over due to the bitterly cold temperatures, and Terry hit the ice with a thud. In a dazed state, he eventually skidded to a halt.

All of the children who were present on Primrose Hill watched the whole spectacle in amazement and then they burst into fits of laughter. But, suddenly, the thinner ice where Terry had landed began to crack and the laughter died away as Terry slid into the icy water. At that point, Amanda realised that if they did not get him out of the pond straight away he would slip further below the ice and freeze to death. Therefore, as fast as lightning, she grabbed hold of her toboggan and rapidly pushed herself across the icy surface as she sped in the direction of the helpless bully. She was also aware that the rescue mission could be very dangerous because the ice could crack further and swallow her up as well, but there was no other option available. Upon reaching the stricken boy, she grabbed hold of his hand and tried to pull him from the water but he was too heavy for her.

"Do something Skelly," Amanda shouted, "…and hurry!"

Skelly immediately popped out both of his arms from his toboggan shape, grabbing Terry just before his head disappeared beneath the water, and he plucked the boy to the safety of the toboggan. After that, they rapidly returned to the snow-covered banks of the pond. It appeared that the rescue mission had been a success but Terry was shivering continuously and his teeth were chattering, which meant that there was now the added danger of hypothermia setting in. So, disregarding any thoughts about her own well-being, Amanda took off her warm coat and threw it over him, realising that she now had to get him back to some warmer surroundings and get him out of his wet clothes. With Terry bundled up in her coat and curled up on the toboggan she dragged him through the snow and took him to her parents' house. During the trek home it began to snow heavily and, by the time they arrived, it was a raging blizzard.

Exhausted and out of breath, Amanda feebly knocked on the front door. Her mother was initially horrified by the appearance of the two frozen, snow-covered specimens but she swiftly took control of the situation. Very soon, Terry and Amanda were huddled in front of the fire in the sitting room, swathed in warm blankets and drinking hot chicken soup.

The weather was so bad for the next two days that they became snowed in, which meant that Terry's parents could not collect him and Amanda's parents could not take him home either because their cars were stuck in deep snowdrifts on their driveways. To Amanda's dismay Terry had to stay in the guest room at her house but, during this time, they became good friends and Terry vowed never to bully Amanda – or anyone else for that matter – ever again.

It seemed that Terry Bull had finally learned his lesson after Amanda had saved his life because he was aware that if it had not been for her quick thinking he would never have survived. Terry felt that he was at least in her debt for that alone. He apologised profusely for his misgivings and begged for her forgiveness. Amanda readily forgave him, of course, and the only bad thing to come out of this event was an extremely nasty cold that Terry managed to catch through his own fault!

CHAPTER FIFTEEN

Skelly Reveals His True Identity

During a particularly mild bout of winter weather Skelly found that he needed to drink much larger quantities of milk than was usual at this time of year. This was because the warmer weather made him feel so much thirstier. However, he had become rather lazy of late and, instead of going out in search of the white liquid, it was far easier for him to take milk from his own doorstep. Therefore, a higher volume of milk than normal was disappearing from Amanda's household. This really incensed Amanda's mother, so she decided to set another trap, determined that she would finally catch the elusive Milk Bandit this time around.

One evening during this mild spell of weather, Amanda's mum went outside and spread black treacle all over the ground, surrounding the area where Dave the milkman always placed the milk bottles. She assumed that the Milk Bandit would get caught up in the gooey mess and would become stuck fast. But, unfortunately, the weather changed that very night as a cold, icy front blew in to cause the black treacle to freeze solid, which turned the surface into a virtual skating rink.

On the following morning Mum arose at the crack of dawn. Then she lay in wait for the milkman to arrive and deposit the milk, after which time she knew it would not be very long before the Milk Bandit showed his greedy little face. She heard the milk float trundling along the lane and, hiding behind a nearby bush, she prepared herself for Dave's departure and the inevitable appearance of the thief. But then it all went horribly wrong because, when Dave's milk float made contact with the frozen treacle, the wheels began to spin around and around like a demented thing until he lost control of the vehicle. Desperately trying to steer his three-wheeled vehicle back on course, Dave fought hard with the steering wheel, turning first one way and then the other, but all to no avail. He spun hopelessly around in circles until his milk float came to an abrupt halt as he hit the grass verge, and then it rolled over onto its side.

The poor, unsuspecting milkman was instantly flung from his cab and thrown into the very bush where Amanda's mum was hiding, whereupon he landed right on top of her whilst being showered with milk bottles that smashed all around them. To cap it all, half-a-dozen eggs then came crashing down on Mum's head. Dave was now on first name terms with her and he was no longer surprised by her hair-brained schemes to try to capture the Milk Bandit.

"Mornin' Janet," said Dave in a casual voice, when the dust and debris began to settle.

"Hello Dave," she mumbled as she spat out pieces of eggshell.

For the next few moments they sat side by side in a sea of milk and broken eggs, with Dave beaming from ear to ear as he watched several egg yolks trickle slowly down her face. Then they both attempted to stand up, but every time the hapless pair tried to take a step they quickly fell over again on the slippery surface beneath them. Eventually, the pair of them decided to slither through the foul-smelling mess until they reached dry ground where Dave managed to get to his feet first. He removed his hat and, looking back at the scene of devastation, idly scratched his head.

"S'a bit of a mess missus – ain't it?" he said with a sigh.

Mum had no option but to agree with him.

"Oh well, s'no using crying over spilt milk, eh? Spilt milk... Get it?" he chuckled as he nudged her.

"I don't think that this is a laughing matter Dave," she said in a rather irritated voice.

Then, after hurriedly apologising for her dreadful mistake she stormed back to her house, aware that her carefully-thought-out plan had gone terribly wrong once again. She felt extremely embarrassed and knew that her husband and daughter would ridicule her for her latest miserable failure but, worse still, when news got out about this event she was bound to be the laughing stock of the entire village.

It took a full day for the milk float to be recovered and for the Environment Agency to clear up the mess that had been caused by her foolish stunt. And, just as she thought, news of the disaster quickly spread around the village like wildfire. On top of all that, Amanda's mum made the headlines in several newspapers as well as on local radio and television. So, because she felt so ashamed of herself, she decided to disappear for a few days until the affair had all blown over. In order to spare her family any further embarrassment Mum decided to take Amanda away too; but, in their haste to depart, Amanda forgot to take Skelly with her.

When they had gone, poor Skelly thought that he had been abandoned. Amanda had left him in his backpack form in the kitchen, on a dining chair beside the table, and there he would have to stay until the weekend was over and Amanda eventually returned home. Skelly's only consolation – or so he thought – was that at least he would be near to the refrigerator where he could easily help himself to milk. However, he was not to know that Amanda's father did not drink milk and he was certainly not aware that the milk order had been cancelled until after the weekend.

On Saturday morning Amanda's dad entered the kitchen, carrying piles of paperwork that he needed to attend to which he normally did in his study. However, he was taking full advantage of the fact that he had the whole house to himself, therefore deciding to spread out a little. Before he sat himself down, Dad picked up the backpack off the dining chair and – after holding it aloft to study it in great detail – he placed it on the floor beside the radiator. Skelly could not understand why Amanda's father had chosen to sit in that particular chair because there were three other chairs around the table, and now he felt uncomfortable after being moved to such a hot spot.

During the previous night Skelly had drunk the remainder of the milk that had been left behind in the refrigerator, and he hoped and prayed that it would be sufficient to make his white colouring last out for the weekend or else he would give away his secret. Under normal circumstances his colouring probably would have lasted but, unfortunately, the extreme heat from the radiator was causing Skelly to perspire and droplets of milk were beginning to form a small pool on the floor beside him. He desperately wanted to get up and move away from the radiator to a cooler place but he dared not because Amanda's father would notice that he had moved. As it turned out, a short while after Skelly had been repositioned beside the radiator, the small pool of milk on the kitchen floor was spotted anyway.

"How odd!" Dad exclaimed out loud.

After making this remark he got up from his chair, picked up a floor-cloth and mopped up the milky puddle. Then he sat down again to resume his paperwork, thinking no more of it.

Meanwhile, Skelly was getting hotter and hotter beside the radiator and he continued to sweat beads of milk. Of course, it was only a matter of time before the fresh puddle of milk was also noticed. With a puzzled expression on his face Amanda's dad put down his pen, reached his arm out towards Skelly and squeezed the backpack between his finger and thumb, noting that milk also oozed from small pores in the material when he did this.

"Hmmph!" he snorted in a questioning tone of voice. Then he stood up and went out of the room.

When he returned Dad carried a large hypodermic syringe in his hand that was fitted with an extremely long needle and, inevitably, a sharp point. As the man bent down he grabbed Skelly by his shoulder strap with his one free hand whilst aiming the needle at Skelly's behind, but before he could insert the needle Skelly quickly sank his teeth into Dad's hand.

"OH NO YOU DON'T!" shrieked Skelly, just before he bit him.

Amanda's father let out a yelp of pain as soon as he was bitten and then another one when he accidentally pierced his own hand with the needle. At the same time, he fell backwards in surprise as Skelly transformed into his alien life-form.

"Uh-oh," Skelly mumbled out loud, "I'm in trouble now!"

He had never revealed his true identity to an adult before, and he did not know what the consequences were going to be for this mistake, but on this occasion Skelly felt that he had to retaliate because he hated needles. For the next few moments the bewildered man simply stared at Skelly in disbelief and then he retreated to the kitchen to cleanse both of his wounds. Once he had finished doing this, instead of calling the police or anyone else that may possibly have been of assistance to him, Dad sat down on a chair and gave Skelly a long, hard stare.

"I wasn't trying to hurt you," he said at length. "I just wanted a sample of your jelly-like flesh so that I could analyse it."

"Oh," said Skelly, "I see; but I thought..."

"And you talk too!" Dad interrupted.

"Yes, of course I do... But why did you want a sample of my flesh?"

"Well, from the moment that I first set eyes on Amanda's new backpack I realised that something wasn't quite right. There was something quite abnormal about you... er, I mean, it."

"Something abnormal about me? Huh! Have you looked in the mirror lately?" said Skelly rather indignantly.

"I didn't mean to offend you. By that last remark I simply meant to say that your texture was different. It is like nothing that I have ever seen here on Earth before – and, believe me, I've studied a few unusual substances."

"Well, now that you've seen me in the flesh you won't have to take a sample, will you?" said Skelly. "And I suspect that I am probably the most unusual thing you have ever seen too Bill... er, Dad... um... I feel like I know you already, having hung around the house for so long, so would you mind if I called you Bill?"

"No, go right ahead," Dad said with a chuckle, "after all, that is my name."

"So, what do you make of me now that you have seen my true identity?" asked Skelly.

"Well, first impressions: you're obviously not from around here, that's plain to see... Mind you, having seen some of the locals, there is a distinct possibility that you could be from around these parts!"

Skelly laughed at this remark and he thought how right Amanda was when she said that her father had a good sense of humour, as well as having the knack of making people feel more at ease. Because he was feeling more relaxed in the presence of this man, Skelly then took the time to explain the whole situation of how he had arrived on Earth and what he had been up to since his arrival. Afterwards, Amanda's dad made a special trip to the village store in order to purchase enough milk to tide Skelly over until deliveries were to be resumed on Monday morning. Then they spent the entire weekend discussing matters in great depth, whilst Skelly roamed freely around the house.

It had come to Dad's attention that every time Skelly walked past the microwave oven in the kitchen he would momentarily pause to stare at it, so he asked him why he did this. Skelly explained that the rays emitted from the microwave oven were visible to his naked eye, although humans could not see them, and this reminded him of Laktose because all waves were part of the electromagnetic spectrum – with gamma rays being the primary source of power used to propel a space-egg. However, he said that these rays were not invented on Earth when he crash-landed all those years ago or else he may have been able to return to his own planet long before now. Having heard Skelly's fascinating story and after giving his plight some careful thought, Amanda's father told him that there was a chance he would be able to assist him with his return to Laktose.

It turned out that Dad did not get his paperwork done after all and, before he knew it, Amanda and her mother had returned from their weekend in exile. Amanda was really pleased to be reunited with Skelly and she remarked on how healthy and well-fed he appeared, considering that the milk order had been cancelled for the weekend. Skelly longed to tell her that he had accidentally revealed himself to her father but he had promised the man that he would not mention a word of it until the appropriate time.

For the duration of the following week Amanda's father had to stay away from home because he was working on a major new project. However, he made a telephone call during the middle part of the week to inform Amanda that he would be taking her to London for a surprise leaving party which was to be held over the forthcoming weekend.

Amanda was delighted at the prospect of this and she looked forward to the party with eager anticipation, at the same time wondering whom the leaving party was in aid of. She was also slightly puzzled by her father's parting remark because he had told her to bring her rabbit-shaped backpack on the trip to London. But, after she had put the telephone down, she thought no more about it.

CHAPTER SIXTEEN

The Big Send Off

On Friday afternoon Amanda's father returned home after his week's absence, whereupon he informed her that they would be departing for London later that evening. Unfortunately, her mother had a pre-arranged event to attend at the Darwood Women's Guild that night and she would not be going with them. Amanda was thus given the responsibility of packing her own suitcase, which she had never had to do before, so she was not really sure what clothes she would need to take with her. All the same, she managed to fill her suitcase until it was almost overflowing, and packed her best party dress just in case. Then, at five o'clock, Amanda and her father set off in his car.

"Where are we going to stay tonight?" Amanda asked as they got into the car.

"We're going to be spending the night in a posh hotel, and then we are going to a farewell party for a close friend of ours tomorrow," her father replied.

"But who, exactly, is this friend?"

"It's a surprise – You'll find out when we get there. Now, do you have your seatbelt on in the back there?"

"Yes," Amanda replied.

"And what about you Skelly? Do you have your seatbelt on too?" he asked.

"Yes," said Skelly, and he immediately began to transform from his backpack shape into his alien life-form.

Amanda's mouth fell wide open in astonishment.

"*SKELLY!*" she gasped. "What do you think you are doing? Now you have given the game away!"

"I'm making myself comfortable," Skelly replied, and then he and Amanda's father began to laugh loudly.

"Don't panic Amanda – I already know all about your little friend and I promise that I won't tell another soul," her father assured her.

"*Dad!* How could you? Why didn't you tell me that you knew Skelly's secret?" Amanda said in disgust.

"I have only known that he existed for a short while, although I have had my suspicions for some time. I realised that you would be too excited for words if I let on and you wouldn't have been able to contain yourself, so I thought it was best to keep quiet until the three of us were all alone," Dad explained.

"It really is okay that your dad is in on our secret because I trust him," Skelly reassured Amanda as he hugged her. "Besides, he might be able to help me return to Laktose."

The ensuing journey to London was a very pleasant one, with Skelly and Amanda relating tales of their many adventures they had shared together, and in no time at all they arrived at their hotel. It was a very posh hotel with fancy décor that included huge crystal chandeliers which hung low from the vast ceilings, beautiful upholstery that was finished in plush black leather, and lovely soft carpets – the pile of which was so thick that Amanda could not even see her shoelaces.

"Wow! How can we afford to stay here Dad?" Amanda asked in an excited voice. "This place is just fantastic, and it must be one of the most expensive hotels in the entire city – or even the most expensive one in the World!"

"Not quite… although it is actually *the* most expensive hotel in London," Dad told her. "However, the company I work for is paying the bill because, although we are going to be having fun, this is really a working weekend for me in the name of research."

Amanda did not really understand what her father meant by that comment and neither did she attempt to question it. Instead, she made the most of the evening, enjoying a fabulous dinner that was served by the most immaculately dressed waiters she had ever seen. Then, after the slap-up meal, Amanda and her father retired to their hotel room for the night.

"Get a good night's sleep," said her dad as he tucked up Amanda in her bed. "Tomorrow is going to be a big day for all of us, so sleep well, and sweet dreams." Then he kissed her lovingly on her cheek.

"You too Skelly – sleep well... And don't sit up all night talking!" he said as he closed the bedroom door.

But, of course, they were both extremely excited in their fancy new surroundings and they did talk for a while. Skelly sat down on the windowsill before he went to his bed, peering longingly out of the window at the night sky and imagining that he was back on his home planet. It was a clear, starry night but, because of the reflection caused by the street lamps against the sky over the big city, all that could be seen was a fluorescent orange glow. Amanda seemed to realise what her little friend was thinking about while he sat there pondering.

"One day Skelly…" she murmured as she drifted off to sleep. "One of these days you will be going home, I promise you that."

But, little did she realise, that day was nearer than she imagined.

The next day was Saturday and the weather was really good. At eight o'clock in the morning it was already bright and sunny, although there was a bitterly cold wind. To start the day, Amanda and her father ate a full English breakfast at their hotel whilst Skelly consumed an enormous glass of milk before they all set off across the city. It took a long time to get to Dad's workplace because the traffic was so heavy and it made Amanda feel glad she was just visiting the city and that she did not have to live there any more.

Amanda had never been to her father's place of work before, so she could only imagine the huge office block where he worked – it might even be a skyscraper, she thought. The car eventually pulled off the main streets and then stopped at a checkpoint, where her father was asked a lot of questions by the security guard before they were allowed to continue. Once the barrier had been raised they travelled along a narrow road, bordered by well-manicured lawns that reminded Amanda of a municipal park, until they passed beneath an archway that led into a spacious courtyard. Then her dad parked his car in the courtyard and turned the key in order to switch off the car's ignition system.

Amanda looked around her at the oblong-shaped, red-bricked buildings that surrounded the courtyard, which seemed quite ordinary-looking and stood just two storeys high. She felt very disappointed that it was neither an office complex nor a skyscraper because she had been really looking forward to climbing a tower block where she would get a good view of the city. Then she spotted a sign over the archway:

'LABORATORIES FOR INTERSTELLAR RESEARCH', it said, in large capital letters.

"Why are we stopping here?" Amanda enquired.

"Because this is where I work," her father replied.

"But I thought you worked in an office – I don't understand," she grumbled.

"Ah, well this is my little secret," said Dad. "You see, I am actually one of the foremost Top Secret scientists in the country. Not even your mother knows that I am a scientist, so she is going to have the surprise of her life when she eventually finds out."

Amanda stared at him in amazement, hardly believing all that her father was telling her.

"When are you going to tell Mum?" she asked.

In reply to that, her father simply winked at her.

"What does 'Interstellar' mean?" Amanda said after a short pause.

"It concerns the stars and anything that occurs in between," Skelly told her. "You know: outer space, the galaxy, undiscovered planets and all that sort of stuff."

"Wow! That's amazing," gasped Amanda.

"And here comes the big one…" said her father, "…Today, we are going to send Skelly back to where he belongs!"

"*CAN YOU DO THAT?*" asked Skelly and Amanda in harmony.

"I believe so. Something like this has never been tried before but we can certainly give it our best shot at the very least."

"How are you going to send Skelly back? We don't have his space-egg," said Amanda.

"Wait and see. All will be revealed this afternoon. In the meantime, you have to go and get changed into your party dress."

Amanda's father took them into the entrance foyer of the building and found a suitable room in which his daughter could change her clothes. She emerged just a short while later looking like the belle of the ball.

"You look very pretty Amanda," Skelly complimented her. Then he placed two fingers in his mouth and blew a loud wolf-whistle.

As Amanda blushed slightly at this, she noticed that Skelly had made an effort too – because he had attempted to flatten down the tuft of fibre-optic hair on top of his head.

"Thank you Skelly," she said. "You don't look too bad either."

"Come along you two," said Amanda's father with a big grin on his face. "There's no time to waste because the party will start very soon and we have to be there."

He hurriedly led them along a lengthy corridor that ended with a pair of panelled oak doors which he unlocked and flung wide open. After ushering Amanda and Skelly inside, he then shut the doors behind them to leave the three of them in total darkness.

"Let the party begin!" Dad suddenly shouted at the top of his voice and, at the same moment, he flicked several light switches in quick succession. This was followed by an immediate chorus of "SURPRISE, SURPRISE," and – much to Amanda and Skelly's astonishment – there stood Ted Peabody and Dave the milkman.

"What are you both doing here?" asked Amanda, and she quickly turned towards her father to complain.

"Dad, I thought you weren't going to tell anybody about Skelly!" she snapped.

"I didn't tell them... they already knew that he existed," her father calmly informed her.

"As you are already aware, I met Skelly years ago," explained Ted, "and that is what prompted me to take up a career as a scientist."

"And Oi 'ave known for years that 'e existed," said the beaming milkman. "At times Oi 'as even caught a glimpse of 'im as well. An' sometimes Oi 'ave left an extra pint of milk for 'im so that 'e never went thirsty."

"Now I understand why you winked at me that day and told me that my mum would never catch him," said Amanda. "You already knew that the Milk Bandit was real!"

Dave nodded his head to acknowledge that she was correct.

"Therefore, I thought it only appropriate to invite these two fine gentlemen to be present at Skelly's Farewell Party," added Amanda's father.

"So, this is what you meant by a leaving party for a close friend," chuckled Amanda. "I'm so glad that I brought my best party dress with me."

"Now that the explanations are over we can start the party," said Amanda's father, eagerly rubbing his hands together. But, before he could go any further, there was a loud knock on the panelled doors.

"Ah, that will be our surprise guest arriving," he announced as he walked towards the doors. "I hope you don't mind, Amanda, but I took the liberty of inviting..." then he paused in mid-sentence to shout out the word "ENTER," at which moment the doors immediately opened into the room.

"...*your mother!*" Dad finished.

"What the blazes is going on Bill?" said his wife as she strode purposefully into the room. Then, all of a sudden, she stopped dead when she saw the small gathering.

"I sent a limousine to collect her," Amanda's father explained to the guests, "because I thought it was only fair that she knew."

Although they remained silent, everyone nodded their heads in agreement of this.

"Who... what is that c-c-creature over there?" asked Mum in a voice that had taken on the tone of someone who had just seen a ghost.

"He's not a creature, he's a being," they all said in perfect harmony.

"And 'e is also the Milk Bandit," Dave said, following up this revelation with a huge guffaw.

"*What?* He's the Milk Bandit!" said Amanda's mum in a wobbly voice. "Oh, I feel as if I'm going to faint."

Dad immediately guided his wife to a comfortable chair where he sat the shocked woman down, handed her a glass of water and began to give her an explanation that covered every aspect concerning Skelly. She listened intently to her husband as the colour slowly returned to her face and, by the time he had told her everything, Amanda's mum was fully relaxed and back to her normal self.

"Well, it is all quite hard to take in," she said after her husband had finished telling all, "and who would have believed that the Milk Bandit was actually an alien from outer space, let alone that my husband was a Top Secret scientist... Well I never!"

After saying this, she got up from her armchair and held out her hand towards Skelly.

"Nice to meet you Skelly," she said with a smile. "I am so pleased to be part of this send-off – I never would have forgiven anyone here if I hadn't been invited."

"It's nice to meet you too, Mrs James," Skelly replied, but he did not dare ask if he could call her by her first name because he thought he might be pushing his luck a little too far.

Then Amanda's mum turned to face Dave the milkman.

"It seems that I owe you a massive apology Dave, for all the hardship I have caused you in my quest to capture the Milk Bandit."

"Like Oi've told yer before missus, forget all about it… C'mon, let's get partying an' see this little fella off with a bang."

"Good call," agreed Amanda's father. "I will arrange for the food to be brought in immediately."

He placed his index finger on a brass button that was situated beside the panelled doors and, within seconds, a troupe of men arrived – all dressed in long white coats and carrying silver salvers stacked high with food – who could easily have been a combination of waiters and doctors.

"These are our caterers for the day," Amanda's father explained, "but don't let anyone worry about them having seen Skelly because they are also Top Secret scientists – we couldn't take the risk of having real caterers in, of course."

The men in white laid out the feast on a long banqueting table at which the guests were to be seated, whereupon they were confronted with a fine spread of edible delights that included savoury snacks, fruit jelly and ice-cream, blancmange and cakes galore, to name but a few. There was also an assortment of drinks consisting of just about every colour in a rainbow. Skelly pointed to these multi-coloured liquids in bewilderment.

"What are these?" he asked nobody in particular.

"These, my friend, are flavoured milks," said Dave. "Oi thought yer moight like t'try something different for a change."

Skelly took a gulp from the chocolate flavoured milk first of all and his flesh instantly turned a shade of brown. When he tried the strawberry flavour, his flesh turned pink. Finally, he sampled the banana flavour, which transformed his skin tone into a shade of light yellow. This whole series of changes tickled everyone and they all began to chuckle. For an encore, Skelly decided to show off and take

169

a gulp of each flavour, one after the other, which gave his flesh a multi-coloured, striped effect... and how everyone laughed at that.

"Remarkable!" muttered Amanda's father as he jotted down notes in a small notepad.

There was much rejoicing and a fun time was had by all as the party went with a swing, but all good things must come to an end and Amanda's father was eventually forced to interrupt the proceedings.

"Ladies and Gentlemen," he bellowed. "Sadly, the time has now come for us to enter The Room of Interstellar Activity... Please follow me."

He unlocked another pair of panelled oak doors at the far end of the banqueting hall and the small group were invited to enter. Here was another room of immense proportions, in the centre of which stood six giant telescopic instruments, positioned in such a way that they were all pointing towards a small platform covered with a tarpaulin. High above this platform there was a dome-shaped roof which contained a massive glass skylight.

"And now for the *piece de resistance,*" said Dad as he swiftly whisked the tarpaulin from the centre platform, in response to which Amanda and Skelly instantly gasped in amazement.

"THE SPACE-EGG!" they exclaimed.

"So that's what a space-egg looks like," echoed Amanda's mum and Dave the milkman at precisely the same moment.

"What is it exactly?" asked Mum.

"It's a travelling capsule," Ted informed her. "I'll explain the finer details to you later on."

"How did you manage to get it, Dad?" Amanda asked. "The last time I set eyes on it, the space-egg was hanging on the wall in the museum!"

"Ah, my Dear... When you have a job like mine it is possible to obtain anything. All I have to do is exert my authority by showing my credentials and then I tell people it is in the interests of humanity that the goods have to be put in my charge – It's as simple as that."

"But how did you know where it was?"

"Well, after Skelly had explained his plight to me when you and your mum went away for that weekend, I had a word with Ted because Skelly knew his space-egg was in a museum but he didn't know where the museum was. It turned out that you had already asked Ted for his help to get hold of the spacecraft and he did some research to locate the exact museum where the exhibit was on show."

"Will it still work after all these years?" asked Dave. "Oi mean, 'cause it wuz buried below the ground fer so long, it must've gone rotten by now."

"On the contrary my friend", said Amanda's father. "The interior of the space-egg is like brand new, just as it was on the day that Skelly travelled into Earth's orbit all those years ago. Mind you, the outer casing was slightly damaged during the impact. However, when it crash-landed, a substance that is wholly unknown on our planet automatically sealed the two halves together in order to protect the interior – A very clever idea indeed. Anyway, to cut a long story short, after a little maintenance the space-egg is now fully-functional and ready to go."

The conversation was beginning to baffle Dave somewhat, so he changed the subject slightly.

"What are those huge telescopes?" he asked.

"Those telescopes are in fact lasers," Dad corrected him. "Basically, they work on the same principle as a microwave oven but we will utilise gamma rays instead of microwaves to power Skelly and his space-egg back into orbit. In effect, the whole set-up is a giant microwave which will heat the space-egg's vital internal instruments – without affecting its pilot of course – but will leave the exterior heat-free for the duration of its hypersonic journey."

Having finished this brief explanation, Amanda's father then raised his head and peered through the glass skylight at the night sky. Now that it was early evening, the winter darkness had already come down and shrouded the city.

"We must say our farewells," he said. "Time is of the essence, and it is vital that the space-egg is launched at exactly the correct moment in order for Skelly to reach his destination making use of a particular trajectory."

In sombre mood, the reluctant throng shuffled forward and hugged Skelly in turn.

"Goodbye old friend," said Ted. "It has been a real joy for me to have caught up with you again after all these years."

"Oi'll miss you me little bandit," Dave told Skelly. Then he grinned and handed him two bottles of milk. "Take these with yer mate, you moight be needing 'em on yer journey 'ome."

"It was a short but interesting acquaintance and I'm really glad that we met," said Amanda's father. "Fly safely."

"I am also glad that we met," said Amanda's mum, "but who am I going to chase from now on?"

Amanda was the last member of the group to step forward and, with tears rolling down her cheeks, she gave Skelly the biggest hug of his life. Then she wiped her eyes and brushed the milk tears away from Skelly's eyes too.

"I shall miss you terribly Skelly but I will always remember you," she said. "Please take this with you as a memento."

Skelly took the lock of hair from Amanda and clasped it tightly to his heart – or wherever he thought that his heart was because he had never been really sure!

"I will miss you too Amanda," Skelly told her in a woeful voice, "and I will think of you often. Be brave in my absence and you will be happy."

Skelly walked to his space-egg where Amanda's father was now waiting to secure the spacecraft ready for its departure, and he climbed inside. But, just as the canopy was about to be sealed shut, he delayed matters.

"WAIT!" he yelled.

Everyone stood by patiently while Skelly fumbled around inside the cockpit for a moment or two, before jumping out of his space-egg and running over to Amanda with an object in his hand.

"This is for you Amanda," he said. "It was in my glove-box and I had completely forgotten all about it… It's a fragment of rock from my home planet of Laktose."

Amanda briefly examined the lightweight, hollowed-out white rock and showed her gratitude by giving Skelly another hug. After which, he strolled back to his space-egg, climbed aboard and the two halves were snapped shut behind him.

Everyone then put on protective goggles and crowded behind a smoked-glass screen to watch the launch of the space-egg, while Amanda's father and his team of scientists, who had earlier doubled as waiters, set the co-ordinates using the instrument panel on the laboratory's master controls. The giant lasers instantly became charged with electricity whilst, at the same time, the skylight slowly began to open up. Suddenly, there was a blinding flash of light, followed by a puff of purple-coloured smoke, and the space-egg was catapulted through the open skylight at an immeasurable speed. As it turned out, there was a firework extravaganza taking place in the city at that very moment, so the bright trail left behind by the hypersonic space-egg would merge unnoticed. Within seconds of the launch, the bright dot that could be seen climbing high into the atmosphere grew smaller and dimmer until it disappeared altogether. Skelly had now gone into orbit.

With nothing more that remained to be said or done, the members of the party who had been left behind quietly said their farewells to each other before going their separate ways. Meanwhile, Amanda continued to look upwards, staring into space through the open skylight as if she was half-expecting Skelly to return at any moment because her life already felt empty without him. Mum and Dad bent down towards their daughter to put their arms around her in an effort to console her, and then all three members of the James family hugged each other.

"Skelly has gone Amanda... Now it's time for us to go too," Dad said in a soothing voice. Then, hand-in-hand, all three left the Laboratories for Interstellar Research and went home.

Things were never quite the same in Amanda's household thereafter. For a while she felt lonely without her little alien friend around but she still had her faithful cat Tabs to talk to, even if the animal never gave her so much as a smile when she chatted to her. However, soon after Skelly had departed the stable block was finished and Amanda received a new companion in the form of a beautiful white horse, as promised to her by her parents, which she aptly named 'Milkstar.'

On a clear, starry night, Amanda regularly perched upon her windowsill admiring the night sky while her eyes and thoughts inevitably drifted towards the Milky Way. She would often wonder what Skelly was doing or whether he would ever return to Earth to visit her. And each time she saw a shooting star, Amanda always made a wish: mostly, she wished that Skelly was there with her, while at other times she wished for a crystal ball so that she could see what the future would hold. But, even if those wishes were never to come true, she was certain that she would see him again one way or another.

NOT QUITE THE END

Also by Wolfren Riverstick:

A CAT CALLED IAN

ISBN: 9780955431401   Price: £5.99

"IAN! What kind of name is that for a cat? Who in their right mind would give such a stupid name to a cat?"

"WE WOULD!" chorused Harlequin The Catmaster and his gleeful assistant Gubbins.

When a young boy decides to climb the magnificent oak tree on top of Sunrise Hill he discovers that there is much more to it than first meets the eye. After mysteriously stumbling into the mystical world of Catland, the unruly ten-year-old is whisked into a courtroom where he is punished with the Sentence of Nine Lives in an attempt to make him change the error of his ways…